I Laughed
Until I Cried

I Laughed Until I Cried

The Memoir of an Adopted Child

Vickie Faulkner Adkins

I LAUGHED UNTIL I CRIED
THE MEMOIR OF AN ADOPTED CHILD

NIV
Scripture quotations marked NIV are taken from the Holy Bible, New International Version®. NIV®. Copyright © 1973, 1978, 1984 by International Bible Society. Used by permission of Zondervan. All rights reserved. [Biblica]

iUniverse books may be ordered through booksellers or by contacting:

iUniverse
1663 Liberty Drive
Bloomington, IN 47403
www.iuniverse.com
1-800-Authors (1-800-288-4677)

ISBN: 978-1-5320-7414-1 (sc)
ISBN: 978-1-5320-7489-9 (hc)
ISBN: 978-1-5320-7415-8 (e)

Library of Congress Control Number: 2019906328

Print information available on the last page.

iUniverse rev. date: 06/19/2019

To the memory of my beloved friend
Mary (Pudgy) Shannon-Coker
and
all the others mentioned here who have gone on before me.
They unknowingly provided stories of laughter and tears.

CONTENTS

PREFACE

Both as a child and as an adult, I struggled to overcome deep emotional wounds and abandonment issues. This book brings to light how adopted children can suffer so severely from rejection that they develop an incredible fear of it. In fact, they can be held hostage by it. Their desire to feel lovable and loved is so great, they might respond in ways which could compromise their lives and well-being. Left unattended, unresolved rejection issues can cause irreversible harm.

Those children and adults who strongly seek attention, love, and acceptance tend to overcompensate. That can become a serious problem. For an example, one might jeopardize herself by accepting years of mental and/or physical abuse in a secret relentless effort to hang on to a harmful relationship. They do that and tell no one because the fear of losing one more person can be greater than all other fears combined.

They are told—or convince themselves—that no one else would want them. Where would they go? Weren't they lucky to have found someone who would take them in the first place? Their own parents didn't care enough to keep them. Surely no one else could. The adopted parents said, "We didn't *have* to take you; we *chose* you. You're special." Didn't that mean their biological parents had exercised some option *not* to keep them? What was really wrong with them? Poor self-esteem, perhaps guilt and shame, meant if abuse did exist, it was probably deserved and never spoken of, certainly not reported.

My Christian counselor told me, "Withholding love is a form of abuse." I have concluded that it is part of the abusive parent's game, whether the biological or adoptive parent. Withhold love so the child keeps struggling for it. It keeps them "in line." Since we are creatures of habit, the behavior we become familiar with as children sets us up to continue making poor choices in adult relationships.

Trained professionals, familiar with the insecure and emotionally traumatized personality, can usually read signs of abuse. A child might act out with poor behavior. Isn't bad attention better than no attention? Worse, the abused can feel so depressed and devalued that he or she might take extreme measures to put an end to the pain. And it is very real pain. Adoptees need to know that it is not possible to escape all the normal feelings that can come with adoption and that's okay. If professional help is needed along the way, that's okay too. They need and must have a safe place to talk freely.

My life and research of my past provided me with the information needed to write this inspirational memoir. Unlike some books in this field of study, criticized for being too depressing, this one is told with enough humor (albeit dark at times) to balance the heavy subject matter. Furthermore, it should help lighten the adoptees' emotional load as they strive to determine why they feel, think, and act the way they do. My intention is to share a way to replace negative thoughts, feelings, and behaviors with freedom and peace through the discovery of truth and the power of forgiveness. Only then can true healing begin. If healing does not come from deep within the heart and soul, it is just another Band-Aid or cover-up—a false face, a mask.

Carol Burnett once said, "Comedy is tragedy plus time." I believe that to be true, determined by how we process what we've been through. I think the comedy that Carol Burnett mentions could be one of those tragic-clown stories. You will find one of those in my own memoir.

And just when I completely understand the irony of the sad clown, I doubt myself.

INTRODUCTION

I Laughed Until I Cried: The Memoir of an Adopted Child casts new light on illegal adoption. Every year, countless children are stolen and sold in the United States and abroad. TV segments of *60 Minutes* and *Unsolved Mysteries* have been dedicated to the atrocity and those who have been affected. I was one of them. My father, like many copycats inspired by baby broker Georgia Tann, who sold more than five thousand children between the 1920s and 1950s, decided to cash *me* in for a quick buck.

Have you ever thought about how your life would be different had you been raised by a different family? Adoption is more common than most people realize. About 60 percent of Americans have a personal connection to it. They were adopted, have adopted, or know someone who was. But that's not why so many are intrigued by adoption. It is because nothing defines our fate more than family. As a result, we're fascinated by stories about people born into one family who, usually through no fault of their own, end up with another.

My story is especially fascinating because my birth mother never gave up on the idea of reuniting her family, and my birth father gave a pretty convincing rendition of how he "never signed any adoption papers." Nevertheless, I *did* end up with another family, and the questionable circumstances did serve to define my fate. Both biological parents faded in and out of my life through adulthood, leaving behind mixed feelings, a multitude of unanswered questions, and no idea how to cope with growing up in what felt like prison with Mommie Dearest as the warden.

This is my story. It chronicles my terrific and tumultuous journey from birth through the development of my life, which now feels more like a predestined passage. I was born in Chewalla, Tennessee, in McNairy County. At the age of three, I was kidnapped; taken from family members and siblings; relocated to Houston, Texas; sold; and raised by a prominent family. I was the first child (though not the oldest) of four adopted children, all from different biological families. My new life offered many opportunities. But along with that privileged lifestyle came certain expectations that were sometimes difficult for me to live up to.

Driven by a strong desire to know more about my past, after many years of research, I realized, *Finally, I have everything necessary to create an informative and interesting narrative that might help another.* I began to write and share my experiences, completely unaware that there was much more to the story. The missing part was undoubtedly the most meaningful.

My memoir might have ended there, incomplete and lacking. But out of nowhere came nothing less than a miraculous telephone call that would enhance my life and change my story forever. That phone call was the key that unlocked a decades-old hidden secret. The discovery resulted in two additional chapters. I want to share my good fortune and my findings. That said, I promise a Hollywood ending, better than anything a screenwriter could come up with.

My voice was silenced for many years. It has taken a lifetime for me to break the emotional link that bound and constrained me. I have discovered that finding our voice sets us free to find and accept truth that longs to be told and needs to be heard so that healing and forgiveness can begin.

> Then you will know the truth, and the
> truth will set you free. (Jn 8:32)

Without knowing your past you cannot know your future, because your future will be the child of your past.

— Osho

CHAPTER 1

Taken

Aunt Doris told me about the day I was born, October 19, 1948.

"Where did that red hair come from, Gloria?" my father asked my mother.

Dr. Smith held me up for my father to have a closer look.

"I asked you, where did that red hair come from? Nobody in either of our families has red hair!" My father's features hardened into a scowl.

The mood in the room changed from excited expectation to doubt and confusion.

Russ Hamilton, a frequent visitor and relative of our next-door neighbor, was sitting on the front porch. Russ was a small man of Native American Indian descent. He looked handsome with his head full of raven-black hair and a dark complexion. Hearing the commotion, he jumped up to look, forgetting that Harold, one of my two-year-old twin brothers, was sitting on his knee.

Harold slid onto the hard floor. He whimpered a little, and his nurturing twin, Jim, gave him a toy to play with.

Aunt Doris said, "Most men shied away from that kind of event, but he seemed very interested. I thought it strange that Russ wanted to be there, especially since he took a quick look and left."

Just minutes before my birth, Aunt Doris had been outside talking with my mother. "Did you decide on a name?"

She answered, "Yes, since my name means glory, if it's a girl, I've decided to name her Vickie, which means victory. If it's a boy, I think I'll name him Kenneth. I've always liked that name."

My mother had a sudden sharp pain and struggled to get up and go inside.

Aunt Doris noticed a wet puddle on the porch step where my mother had been sitting.

She hurried her into the house. "Gloria, didn't you feel your water break?"

My mother had another, sharper, pain that lasted twice as long.

"Gloria, get into bed. I'm going to take a look, see how far along you are." She did a quick examination and exclaimed, "That baby could come at any moment. There's no time to get to the hospital." She stepped around the corner to the living room. "Somebody call the doctor."

How lucky my mother was that Aunt Doris was there that day, strong and full of confidence. Although she's a small woman—a hundred pounds soaking wet—she is a mighty force who believes in herself and her ability to get the job done.

It hadn't been that long since she had given birth to her own baby boy, so she was aware of all the ready signs. She knew it was time and kept repeating, "I can do this." She hurried to gather clean sheets and towels while silently praying for the doctor's quick arrival.

"Gloria, where are your clean linens?" Aunt Doris shouted from the bathroom.

"Bathroom cabinet; that's all I have."

Aunt Doris ran out the door and hollered back, "I'm going home to get more." Preoccupied with her thoughts, she ran straight out into the street.

A car zipped past, swerved, and barely missed her.

She went inside her home to gather things she thought might be needed. Just as she was leaving, Uncle Grady asked her to change the baby's diaper. She did that and hurriedly went out the door. Across the street stood the car that had almost hit her, parked in front of the house. She walked in and discovered that the doctor had arrived. She had missed the whole thing.

"Are you deaf? I asked you, where did that damn hair come from?"

Aunt Doris said that my mother, exhausted from having just given birth, chose to ignore him.

Evidently my aunt could read my puzzled look; she offered an explanation. She said, "Some people share an old belief about having a redheaded baby: with red hair being rare, a child born to non-redheaded parents was often assumed to be the child of an affair."

Country folks do have their beliefs.

Apparently that explains why people still joke and say things like "I wonder who the father is" when a redheaded child is born.

I'm not sure whether my hair color had anything to do with what my mother called "the day he went whacko" a few years later.

The two of them were always mad at each other about something: dinner was cold; his shirt wasn't ironed; he made her sick …

They quarreled most of the day. He left. But that time when he left, he shouted, "And I won't be back!"

He slammed the door so hard that I thought the walls had cracked. I looked out the window and watched him speed away, slinging yard mud and road gravel everywhere. I wasn't the only one looking; by then Jim and Harold were standing next to me.

Neighbors were watching too. One threw a full beer can at the car and shouted, "There are kids on this street, you maniac."

Late that night, I woke up thirsty and needed a drink of water. I found my mother sitting in one of the dining room chairs. There was a pencil and a tablet on the table. She got up, went to the kitchen, and brought me a drink. I sat on her lap and asked what was written on the paper. She said, "It's just numbers."

I asked, "Why are there numbers on the paper? What do they mean?"

She smiled and said, "It's just boring old numbers about money and bills; nothing for you to worry about." I saw a tear run down her cheek.

I raised my hand to her face and wiped away the tear. Her white skin was so soft and pretty. I said, "My mommy." That always made her smile.

The smile disappeared when she saw headlights and heard my father's car pull into the yard. Her shoulders tightened and a tense frown replaced the smile when we heard his boots hit the porch.

The door flung open, shuddering on its hinges as the doorknob clanged against the wall behind it. My father wobbled into the door frame and sagged against the wall. His hollow, drunken eyes fell on us. Mother put me down off her lap and stood.

"Ah there she is." My father waved an arm menacingly in our direction. "It's my whore future ex-wife and her bastard child."

"She's your child too, you know," my mother replied softly. She stepped in front of me. I held on to her skirt while peering around her side.

"That little shit is not my child," he snapped, stabbing an accusatory finger in my face.

"Why don't you just go to bed and sleep it off? You're drunk." Mother suggested, her voice gaining an edge.

"Oh, no... no... no. You don't get to tell *me* what to do," he responded through clenched teeth, herding us into the kitchen.

He fumbled with a kitchen drawer, forcing it open and retrieving a butcher knife. Mother's eyes widened in disbelief; she pulled me in front of her and slunk against the cabinets opposite my father. Stark white kitchen lights glinted off the wide stainless steel blade of the knife as he towered over us.

"Maybe I should just kill you, save myself the embarrassment of living in the house with an unfaithful slut." His voice was frighteningly calm, resolved.

"You wouldn't!"

"Wouldn't I? I don't think any judge or jury would blame me, once I let them know what my *wife* has been up to."

Mother picked me up and began sobbing. When she started to cry, so did I. When I began to cry, she became angry that he made me cry. She held me up like a shield and shouted, "You might as well go ahead and kill her too. What kind of life would she have without me?" Terrified and through tears I cried while repeating, "No-no-no-no-no."

Traumatic events like this one are burned into our brains forever. While we may forget the exact words spoken or struggle to remember the exact feelings we felt at the time, we never forget the event itself.

My father didn't come around much after that. Maybe he was afraid of what he might do.

Times got hard for my mother. There was little money coming in. Nothing except the small amount he chose to give her every now and then, if he hadn't spent it all in the bars.

I don't think we could have rented a house any cheaper. The one we lived in wasn't much with its rotten boards and leaky windows, but it managed to keep the rain off our heads most of the time, unless there came a gully washer. Those times, pots and pans caught the water that pounded through the roof.

The floor was a bunch of loose or broken vinyl tiles. The tile had hardened with age, and the glue that once held it together had disintegrated. When my mother swept, the broom moved them around. It looked like some big, ugly checkerboard, with no resemblance to any kind of order. The checkers must have fallen through the cracks. The more she tried to clean, the more dirt appeared. Life can look like that sometimes. When the family unit loses its cohesiveness, it's easy to see how the children from those broken families can fall through the cracks.

The house had a musty smell. My mother, try as she would, couldn't get rid of it. Maybe it was the never-ending pile of dirty clothes on the bathroom floor. They would have to wait there until she collected enough coins and energy to pull a clothes wagon while herding three kids to the Laundromat.

On a pretty day, she opened the windows and turned on our box fan to help circulate the air. The screens were tattered, torn, or missing, so all that did was let in a swarm of flies during the day and mosquitoes at night. We didn't have to worry about a person breaking in. Nobody around had anything to steal, especially not us. Our worst predators were those mosquitoes.

Our house was better than nothing, and our mother couldn't count on my father to give her enough money for food, let alone to fix leaks or floors. She had no idea how next month's rent would get paid and tried hard not to think that far ahead. At times we couldn't buy bare necessities such as bread and milk. One time, she found me sitting in the middle of the kitchen table eating a stick of margarine. It was the only thing left in the refrigerator, and I was hungry.

My mother didn't have parents to help out. Her birth mother died when she was only eight. Her stepmother didn't want to be bothered so she "sent her packin'." Gloria was raised by her daddy's brother, Archie, and his wife, Vinnie—pronounced Vine-e. They were good people, family folks. They didn't have much of anything to brag about. But that didn't matter to Archie and Vinnie. They said, "As long as we have our family, we have everything."

They had heard stories and rumors about the despicable woman named Georgia Tann, over in Memphis, far too close for comfort. Their hearts went out to the victims of her illegal doings. According to the Newton County, Mississippi, Historical and Genealogical Society archives, "From 1924 to 1950, Georgia Tann stole, or otherwise separated more than *five thousand* children from their families." Researchers Lois Cooper and Louise Bailey discovered that "by *1920*, Tann began placing kidnapped children." Georgia began working for Kate McWillie Powers Receiving Home for Children in Jackson, which was affiliated with the Mississippi Children's Home Society. Georgia was run out of Mississippi for her 'child-placing' methods and went to Texas. She then moved to Memphis, Tennessee. "Tann became Executive Director of the Memphis branch of the Tennessee Children's Home Society." That's when her real child trafficking and profiteering began.

Georgia Tann had money and *connections*, which included a judge. In Tennessee, she used them to get the names and addresses of poor white people who signed up for welfare. Then she'd go tell parents how she would help them out by keeping their children until they could get jobs.

She asked them to sign papers, claiming the papers would allow her to take care of their children. She gave convincing reasons such as "in case they get sick and need to see a doctor."

Lots of parents couldn't read, but they were desperate and wanted to believe what she told them. She promised they could come visit their children anytime.

It looked like their only means of help. They *sure* didn't want their children going hungry. Reluctantly, they'd sign or make their X. The next thing they knew, the kid was adopted and sometimes sent off to another state. A few were lucky and got good parents, while others were abused or made to work hard at an early age.

Awful stories were going around—stories about kids who were physically and sexually abused by Georgia, her workers, *and* adoptive parents. Tales were told about how adopted children became little servants and maids. They were made to do things such as wax floors, wash dishes, mow lawns, clean barns, whatever needed doing—no matter their age or size. Later on, people found out the stories and tales were true. Little to no background check was done on new parents. The only thing that mattered to Georgia was whether they could afford her services. She catered to the rich, and many times that included famous Hollywood stars.

That is how the actress Joan Crawford got two of her children. "Tann's black market adoption ring placed children with politicians, millionaires, and celebrities primarily in California and New York. Her celebrity clients included Lana Turner, Mary Pickford, June Allyson, and Joan Crawford," states Philip Jett in his article "Georgia Tann: The Matron of Evil," which appeared online October 25, 2018, @ criminalelement.com. Before writing her book *The Baby Thief*, Barbara Bizantz Raymond conducted extensive research on the subject. The book is a major source of information. Georgia Tann, otherwise known as a "baby broker," became a wealthy woman. Tann convinced herself that she was doing what was best for the kids. She justified her actions by saying, "The children were given financial, educational and cultural opportunities they would not have otherwise had." I guessed it didn't matter whether or not love was part of the equation.

My mother signed up for something called "assistance," where free milk was given to the needy. She filled out an application that asked for the names, ages, and addresses of her children. When my daddy's folks got wind of what she did, they paid us a visit. They came rollin' up into the yard lookin' and soundin' like a bunch of showoffs. The car radio was blaring, and its mufflers were rumbling, drowning out all sounds of an otherwise quiet day. A sickening smell of gasoline hovered over the fresh air. The teenage-actin' *men* hopped out of the car and banged on our door. Jim and Harold ran to see who was there. They pushed past the boys demanding, "Where's your mother?"

Mother walked into the room. She was bombarded with questions.

"What's this I hear about you signing up for welfare?" One of my uncles asked my mother, words dripping with disdain.

"I did what I had to do to provide for my family," Mother replied, shoulders square, chin held high. "Besides, I signed up for assistance, not welfare."

"Wow, Melzar sure can pick 'em!" He laughed. "You're an idiot. Don't you know that *assistance* is just a fancy word for welfare?"

"Call it whatever you want. It means I will be able to feed my children. No thanks to you or any of the Barnes family."

He responded, very loud and serious this time, "No, since you're too dumb to figure it out, I'll tell you what it means. It means that Tann or one of her workers could grab your kids and put them in the illegal orphanage. Then none of us will ever see them again. Maybe *that's* what you *really* want?"

The news of Georgia Tann and her evil, illegal, exploitation of children was spreading in the South. It was impossible for that many kids to disappear unnoticed. That would be almost two hundred children a year even if the same number were taken annually—and I'm pretty sure they weren't. The number seemed to increase as the years went on, and Georgia Tann seemed to get bolder as she became more powerful. Since Mother had provided our address, she was frightened and offered no real resistance when one of them suggested they take the boys to live with our grandparents, Clifford Barnes (Big Daddy) and Eva, his wife. They said I should stay with Uncle Grady and Aunt Doris. "It will only be for a little while; your kids will be safe."

My grandfather owned a sawmill. When Aunt Doris could, she would take me to visit. I spent some time there with my two big brothers and Big Daddy. One time, he had his men place a long board across a huge tree lying on the ground. They made a seesaw for us to play on.

We kids learned how to make homemade grape Kool-Aid popsicles. We poured the liquid into cold metal ice trays and returned them to the freezer. Then, we waited. When the cubes were almost frozen, we placed wooden stick handles in the center of each perfect square. The trays full of purple ice popped and cracked when the handle was lifted. That seesaw and the cold, sweet taste of grape popsicles are a couple of my only memories, more like *flashbacks*, from that time.

I will never forget the aroma of freshly cut wood, which is probably why I still love that smell. Not only is the strong natural scent so good that it offsets the loud, high-pitched, shrill, shrieking noise of chain saws, but it takes me back to a fun time spent with my twin brothers, Jim and Harold.

At one time, Big Daddy owned a company that made cedar chests. I guess he made good money, because he ended up keeping the twins for about eight years. That's when his wife told him, "Gloria needs to come get her boys since she's remarried and doin' okay." Big Daddy called our mother. She and Dale, her new husband, left Michigan and drove to Tennessee to get them.

Meanwhile, I lived with Aunt Doris; Uncle Grady, my father's brother; and Johnny, their son. Aunt Doris took good care of us. Her words made me feel secure and loved. She would say, "Now, I have my little boy and my little girl."

One hot, sunny day, Johnny and I were sitting in the shade under a big tree with Aunt Doris's father. She was picking beans in the garden when someone came running up to the house shouting, "Doris, you have an emergency phone call at the store."

The store was about a mile up the road. Frightened, Aunt Doris jumped into the car and drove.

When she returned, she looked really upset. I asked, "What's wrong, Aunt Doris?"

"That was Gloria on the phone." She addressed her father.

"She found out we are movin' to Texas next week and plan to take Vickie with us."

"Of course you will. Why wouldn't you?" Grandpa replied, incredulously. "What did she say?"

"She threatened me … said, if we do that, she will have us arrested for *kidnappin'* as soon as we cross the Tennessee state line."

That wouldn't have taken but a few minutes since we practically lived at the Tennessee/Mississippi border.

Her father paused, thinking before speaking. "You will have to leave Vickie behind." My heart sank. "If you take the risk, Johnny might have no one to take care of him."

And Johnny needed lots of taking care of. A short time after he was born, he developed whooping cough and encephalitis. The two illnesses left him disabled. Johnny couldn't walk or form words to make sentences.

One day, Aunt Doris thought her child was perfect, and the next day, she was left to pick up the pieces of a tragic reality. It's no wonder she had to be protective of her son, and would be for the rest of her life. From that day forward she became isolated, except for frequent doctor visits with Johnny. I've always considered her the strongest and most patient woman I have ever known.

The next day, my mother's friend came to pick me up. He said he was taking me with him for the day. He was the brother of a minister who had befriended her in past times. I didn't know him at all. Aunt

Doris hated to let me go but could do nothing about it, except get his phone number. By late evening when I had not returned, Uncle Grady told Aunt Doris to go to the store, call, and demand he bring me back home. Uncle Grady said, "Since the man is not a family member, by *law*, he has to bring her back."

I guess Uncle Grady was right, because the man did take me home, but he wasn't happy about it. He practically left me on the doorstep. He knocked on the front door, removed something from his shirt pocket, and handed it to me. Aunt Doris opened the door and watched as he backed out of her driveway. She picked me up and carried me inside.

Years later, I saw a picture of the minister's brother standing on a big porch, holding me in his arms. The picture had been taken the day we spent together. I found it among Aunt Doris's many photos, and I asked her who it was. That's when I learned that the man and his wife had planned on keeping me.

There was another picture of me among Aunt Doris's things. I am standing between two girls. I looked at it for a long time feeling as if I should know exactly who the girls were. Finally, I had to ask about them. Aunt Doris had no recollection of either, but we found their names written on back of the photo: Marilyn and Sandra. I am still unable to remember them but I wish I could. I feel an unexplainable closeness to them.

The next week, someone else came to get me. That person took me to live with my mother's people, Aunt Vinnie and Uncle Archie, the couple who had raised her after her mother died. They had older, identical-twin girls, Lurline and Geraldine, who looked after me. We played house, and I was their little girl. Sometimes we played school, and they would read to me. I loved our time together and all the attention. It was like having two protective big sisters to watch over me.

One night, I begged the twins to pin curl my hair so it would look pretty and curly. They said, "It's too late; it's time for bed, and you shouldn't sleep with your hair wet 'cause you might catcha' cold."

It was many years later when Lurlene and Geraldine, then grown women with families of their own, told me how much they regretted not pin curling my hair that night. That was the last time we saw one another for more than thirty years. In the wee hours of morning, while I slept, my father came to get me.

I woke up when I heard Uncle Archie begging my daddy to leave me with them. My father said, "No."

I was sad to leave the twin girls. If they knew my daddy was coming to get me, I know they would have fixed my hair, but none of us had known. He put me in the car, and I watched out the back window as he drove away. I felt sad enough to cry, but I didn't want to. If he thought I wasn't happy to see him, it might hurt his feelings.

I tried to keep the porch light in sight, in case he changed his mind. Then, I might need to find my way back home in the dark. The farther he drove, the smaller it became. Eventually, the light was a tiny dot, and even that disappeared into the darkness. He was taking me away from everything and everyone I ever knew. He said we would start a new life in Texas. I couldn't fight it—tears began to roll down my cheeks. That's when he said, "Aunt Doris and Johnny are there, in Texas."

I missed them so much. I couldn't wait to see them again.

CHAPTER 2

Vanished

I had no idea where Texas was, but it was great to be reunited with Aunt Doris and Uncle Grady, especially with Johnny. I really loved them, so if this was their home, it was easy for it to be mine.

Uncle Grady got a good job and found one for my father, who had met a woman. My daddy's plan was to get my twin brothers, Jim and Harold, who were back in Tennessee living with our grandparents. Daddy said, "Then we will all be a family."

I was happy with that, especially since we were practically next door to Aunt Doris. I stayed with her every day when he went to work.

Aunt Doris's house was small. It sat in the side yard of the biggest house I had ever seen. The two homes were separated by a fence with a gate which stayed open all the time.

Johnny and I had a swimming pool in the backyard of the big house. It was a vinyl wading pool, but to us, it was the best one in the world. Aunt Doris would fill it with fresh water from the garden hose. Then she would sit on the porch sipping sweet ice cold tea in the hot Texas sun while she watched us play and splash around. The sun highlighted her pretty face. Her dark hair was bright and shiny. I thought she looked like an angel in her white dress, which had the fragrance of being freshly starched and ironed. Hearing her laugh and the sound of ice rattling in her tea glass made a miserable hot summer day in Houston seem almost perfect. She took such good care of Johnny and me. I loved this woman with all my heart. This was my family.

I was sad that my brothers never came to live with us. My father seemed sad when the woman he met went away. But I had Aunt Doris and Johnny. I didn't need anyone else.

One day, my father took me to the big white house next door to Aunt Doris. He knocked on the door. While we waited for someone to answer, he gave me instructions: "Vickie, Doris has to take Johnny to the doctor today. Mrs. Ray, the landlady, said you could stay with her."

"How long?" I asked.

"You should stay there until I come pick you up after work," he replied. "The lady is doing us a favor, so don't give her any trouble, and don't get into any trouble. Whatever you do, do not leave this house. Don't talk too much, and don't ask too many questions, the way you sometimes do."

"Why not?" I asked.

"See, that's what I'm talking about," he answered.

I said, "Okay." We smiled at one another. Then he picked me up and gave me a big hug.

Mrs. Ray came to the door and invited me in. I was surprised to see a woman who was the same height as my daddy.

He put me down and said, "Goodbye." Then he placed his index finger on the tip of my nose and made a quick downward stroke. The gesture and the hug made me feel warm inside. They reassured me about what I was feeling. The two of us were becoming very close.

The landlady's house and surrounding area took up half the block with its huge front, back, and side yards. The front yard faced a busy street with a continuous line of cars coming and going. At one end of the busy street was an industrial area where the steel mill, shipyard, and alloy plant was. That's where both my daddy and Uncle Grady worked. At the other end was a beer joint where men would go after work.

My daddy didn't come to get me that day. When the day turned into night, I lay in bed upstairs in the big house. The window was open, and the sheer curtains danced to Hank Williams singing, "jambalaya, crawfish pie, fillet gumbo ..." Tears filled my eyes. I thought he was probably up the street putting money in the jukebox. That's the song he always played when he took me with him. *Where is he? Has he forgotten me?* Then, the attic fan came on. The curtains stopped dancing and hovered close to the windows. I was glad for the noise of the fan. It helped drown out the sound of the song. I finally went to sleep.

No one came to get me the next day. The lady who owned the house—for that matter, she owned all the ones around—made breakfast. She seemed nice, but I really didn't know her. I didn't talk much. That went on for a few days.

I did not ask questions, but I was very worried. I ran to the closest window every time I thought I heard the sound of a car pull into the long driveway. Many times each day, I walked up the stairs and looked out the front windows and then walked back downstairs and looked out the kitchen window toward the small house, but saw no one. I was beginning to wonder if my father was ever coming back to get me.

There were so many times when I thought a car pulled in. Every single time, I repeated the ritual; upstairs, front window; downstairs, back window. But I never saw Aunt Doris or Johnny.

I saw the lady hanging clean sheets on the clothesline in the backyard. It seemed so high, yet she had no trouble reaching it. She was a large woman, tall and big-boned. I was thinking how Aunt Doris would have to stand on a ladder to hang our clothes on that line. The tall lady was wearing a nice dress and shoes with little heels. The shoes matched the color of her dress. Her hair was short and gray. She wore silver glasses with rhinestones that sparkled like diamonds. That morning, she had wavy silver clamps all over her head. I guessed that when she took them out her hair would look that way, the way mine looked curly when it had been pin curled. Aunt Doris's hair was dark, medium length, and naturally curly.

In a few minutes, the lady came inside, filled a tall soda pop bottle with water, and put the sprinkler-stopper back in. I figured she was getting ready to iron. Instead, she got busy with housework.

I hadn't been up for long, but my mind and body felt tired and ached with pain. Worrying about my family was keeping me awake at night. I tossed and turned and fought frightening thoughts that found their way into my head—thoughts of lost children who can't find their way home and thoughts of people begging for help but dying anyway. One night, I thought I heard the sound of someone screaming.

When morning finally came, I woke up exhausted. When my feet touched the floor, my legs felt shaky and unstable. The nightmares, sleepless nights, and constant trips to the windows, only to be let down over and over again, were wearing me out. I sat in one of the kitchen chairs, pulled my knees up under my chin, rested my head on them, and looked out the screen door.

I watched those sheets as they swayed back and forth. I couldn't quit looking at them. The motion seemed to have a hypnotic effect, and my eyes became fixed on them. I stared for so long that they began to take on a ghostlike appearance. The wooden clothespins began to look like eyes staring back at me. Suddenly, I had an overwhelming forlorn feeling. It took my breath away, and I gasped. Instead of holding me back, it seemed to push me forward. I remembered my promise not to leave the house, *"… and whatever you do, do not leave the landlady's house."* But I *had* to go to the little house and check on Aunt Doris and Johnny. I knew something was very wrong.

I opened the screen and walked out the back door toward Aunt Doris's house. The gate was closed. *That is strange. Is someone trying to keep me from going to the house?* I opened the gate and stepped up onto the porch. I knocked on the door, softly at first; then I began to jiggle the loose black metal door knob back and forth and knocked again, louder that time, but no one came. Disheartened, I slowly headed back to the big house, carefully avoiding the clothesline full of gleaming white fabric.

When I returned, no one was there. Every light in the house was turned off. I called to the lady … no answer. I was scared to death. *Is someone or something taking all the people away from me?* I was shaking and began to cry.

Still crying and afraid, I gathered the nerve to feel my way through the dark house to the front living room. Cautiously, I began the slow walk. First, I went from the big kitchen and felt my way through the dining room. Then I was forced to open the first of two doors, one on each side of the hall. I hesitated for a moment, remembering how frightening it was when I played hide-n-seek with my brothers and kids back home. The older ones jumped out from behind closed doors and scared the bejeebers out of the younger ones. They could always find the best places to hide.

Wait! What if someone is hiding behind this door? How can I get away?

My heart was pounding so hard that I thought it would jump out of my body. Trying not to make a sound, I turned the glass knob and barely cracked open the door. Then I quickly pushed the door wide open. No one there! I peered up the long hallway. It was dark. I could hardly see the two closed doors at the opposite end, one on each side. I called to the lady. Fear made me forget her name. "Lady, are you there?" There was no answer. I was scared, now more afraid of being left alone than anything else.

Continuing on, I crossed the hallway. I prepared myself to open the second door. That door led to the living room at the front of the house. Again, I swung the door open! Not fast enough! I saw a shadow! I jumped and screamed and then cried out, "Mrs. Ray!"

Now, trembling with fear, my hands shaking, I started to cry. The blinds in the room were closed, so there was very little light. What light *did* manage to creep through formed a ray which looked like a straight arrow that shot right through me.

At that moment, I was paralyzed with fear and became frozen in my tracks. By then, my fear was that something evil was lurking nearby. I could feel its presence. I tried to be totally silent, terrified that any noise would bring it forth, and I too would disappear. I held my breath until I thought I would pass out. All of a sudden, the landlady, Mrs. Ray, appeared from her hiding place behind a big chair in the corner of the room.

Startled yet relieved, I ran to her and tried to hug her. She extended her arms, sternly holding me at that distance. She was still on her knees from the crouched hiding position. That enabled her to look directly into my face. She asked, "Where did you go?"

Sobbing, I could barely get the words out. In a quivering, broken voice, I was finally able to answer, "To see Johnny and Aunt Doris, but they weren't there."

She placed her open hands firmly onto my shoulders. She glared at me. Her eyes scared me. They looked cold and angry. In a raised voice, she said, "You *never* leave this house again without my permission. Do you understand?"

I nodded and replied with a soft, sorrowful yes. But I really didn't understand.

I didn't understand any of this. I was only four years old, and they were my family. Now, they were gone. Why wouldn't the lady tell me where they went? This would be the first of many lessons my "new mother" would teach me.

Aunt Doris, Uncle Grady, Johnny, and my father were gone … vanished! I would not see any of them again for many years—at which time I learned my new mother made them move out of her rental house and ordered them to never contact me again, or they would suffer consequences.

It took awhile to get over the initial shock of losing my entire family. I know I never got over the actual loss.

For a long time, I watched the cars drive past the house and hoped that someday one I recognized would stop and turn into our driveway. Aunt Doris would be driving. She'd roll down her window, and there would be a big beautiful smile on her face. Johnny would be in the back seat waving at me with his face pressed against the glass. I'd be so happy because they were coming to take me home. Sometimes, I pretended it happened that way. It was make-believe, but it seemed so real that I could almost feel their presence.

That day never came, and the fading memory became too painful to revisit. I have discovered that if one will allow it, the mind has a way of self-protecting before going on overload, a default option, so to speak. That hadn't been the first of my four-year-old life-altering experiences. The new mother, Mrs. Ray, called them, "shuffled from pillar to post." But at age four, I was old enough to understand a little more and was a lot more attached to the people I had come to love and then lost. The casual cliché fell painfully short of describing my innermost heartfelt feelings.

While it certainly had not been my first loss, it was the most painful of the many I would learn to keep tucked away, deep inside my damaged heart. They could all be stored there and dealt with at some later, healthier time. Dumping the load onto my heart allowed my mind the rest it needed so it could give me permission to move forward. That emotional event was the first brick used to build my own personal heart-protective wall.

It was never a secret that I was an adopted child. How else do you explain being a childless couple one day, and the next day, you have a four-year-old daughter? Besides, there were at least two generation gaps between my new parents and me. I thought life with my adopted family was pretty normal. But what, pray tell, could I possibly have known about normal?

I was like most kids. I had a mama—everybody called her Mrs. Ray; a daddy—they called him Mr. Ray; a grandma—Mama's mother; and an uncle. I called him Unckie. We all lived together in a nice big house with a swing set. Two beautiful black cocker spaniels, Princess and Lizzy, lived in our big yard. They were my two best friends. I could tell all my secrets to Princess. Lizzy was older and not very patient. Sometimes she got jealous and bit Princess.

At age five I went to kindergarten and began to take private piano lessons. On some special Sundays, after we got out of church, my new daddy would take me to the pony rides in Pasadena. It cost ten cents to ride one round or three rounds for a quarter. My daddy knew a good thing when he saw it. I always got to ride three rounds. If it had rained, the circular dirt track was muddy. On those days, the little horses didn't make their usual rounds. They took the day off, and Daddy took a disappointed little girl back home. Lucky for me, the Texas sun usually kept the track dry and sandy. An occasional gust of wind could send the sandy dirt blowing through the air and landing on my clothes but mostly in my long hair.

The ponies were hooked up to something that looked like large spokes. In the center of the spokes, there appeared to be a big wooden wheel. All the ponies could do, all day long, was walk around in a circle. I wondered how they kept from getting dizzy.

I loved being in the saddle with the wind blowing through my hair. I pretended the two of us, my chosen horse and me, were chasing outlaws through town, like in the westerns I watched on television. I wanted to set all of them free so they could run. We would be just like the Lone Ranger and his horse, Silver. I was sure I could call them back to their places by whistling. They looked just as smart as Silver. *I'll bet I could whistle, and not only will they come back, but they will return to their own assigned, pie-shaped, wheel-slot. That's something I need to work on, whistling.*

When Daddy and I returned from the pony rides, Mother would be waiting with a towel. She would say, "Go to the bathroom and get out of those dirty clothes."

She followed behind, wrapped the towel around me, and ordered me to sit on top of the dirty clothes hamper. I looked out the window while I waited. I watched her go outside and fetch a round, white metal pan with a red rim. The pan contained rainwater.

When she came back in, she lifted me up on top of the long, cold pink tile bathroom counter, had me lie on my back, and placed my neck on a homemade rolled-up hand-cloth pillow.

She proceeded to wash my hair in the sink with "special" shampoo. She used the fresh rainwater sparingly, as though each drop was some precious commodity specifically released from heaven to wash and rinse hair stating, "This water is cleaner and doesn't contain any harsh chemicals." *Can we say acid rain?*

That should have been my first clue regarding Mother's strange obsession with my hair. I am certain our drinking water came straight from the tap. If she really believed that assumption, then hair-wash water was more important to her than our drinking water.

My second clue should have come a few days later. That's when she started dying her hair. She colored it red to match mine. The dye smelled as if it contained *lots* of strange chemicals. She didn't seem to mind. She said, "Now we look just alike."

Sometimes for fun, Mother took me to a wonderful, magical place, Kiddyland Park. It opened in Houston, in 1950, and closed in the 1960s. I loved the rides and wished I could stay there forever. She had a hard time getting me to leave. But I knew better than to act too cantankerous, or I might not get to go back.

When I outgrew the rides at Kiddyland, Mother took me to the much larger Playland Park. I felt like I had died and gone to heaven. The music was loud, corn was poppin', and pink cotton candy was being swirled and served. There was a beautiful carrousel with music and jewels and elaborate hand-painted horses, which I rode many times. Mother only allowed me to ride the carrousel, the motor boats, and the bumper cars. I didn't mind. Just walking through that park was like a stroll through paradise.

Playland Park was located at 9200 South Main. It was *the* place to go and to be between 1940 and 1967, when it closed. I doubt there was a kid in Houston during that time who did not visit or at least *know* about Playland Park and all its great rides. There was the Skyrocket, its famous wooden roller coaster; the Bullet, faster than a speeding one; and the popular Tilt-a-Whirl. Oh, and who could ever forget the infamous eerie fortune teller in her glass cage? Her stiff, mechanical arms could shuffle and deal your very own personalized card. Didn't she hold the future in the palm of her hand?

At age six, I continued on to private school for first grade. At seven, I began to prepare, courtesy of Mrs. Hoffman and months of grueling practice, to participate in a piano recital playing "Tales from the Vienna Woods."

The best things about the recital were the pretty, pastel-purple formal dress and jeweled sandals I wore. I loved those sandals. My feet looked like they were covered in clear sparkling diamonds with just a hint of gold trim. The worst thing about the recital was that the dress was made of tulle, an itchy material which made me scratch.

I watched my mother's smile deteriorate into a look of disgust when I scratched and hit the wrong notes and chords.

She exaggerated the error by covering her ears with both hands.

I loved the piano, if someone else was playing, but hated practicing. It took five years of fruitless lessons (but only that one recital) to convince my mother that I would never be a Liberace, whom she idolized.

I loved my school teacher, Ms. Tanner.

Ms. Tanner loved the arts and taught private school and private acting lessons. That is when I developed a desire to act. It is also when Ms. Tanner, courtesy to my mother, who had a desire for me to lose the Tennessee dialect so she would not be further humiliated in public, taught me the art of proper "e-nun-ci-a-tion."

Mother signed me up for diction lessons and whispered somethin' to Ms. Tanner about someone named Eliza Doolittle. That's when they both smiled real big. I thought I heard them say this Eliza person had a pig, a male pig. He was really old, an eon. I don't think I was supposed to have overheard any of that because they were talking behind their hands. I guessed I was getting a pet pig. It was going to be a surprise. I ruined it by listenin' in. Now, I would have to act surprised so Mother wouldn't be angry with me. I hoped it wouldn't be that old male pig of Eliza Doolittle's. I would have preferred a puppy or a kitten, but the old pig was probably free.

When it was time to buy school clothes, Mother took me downtown to shop at Foley's. Mother paid the clerk with a silver metal card. She slid it out of a leather-looking holder. She called it her charge card. I thought the height of success would be to own one of those powerful cards. I would purchase all the moving dolls in the windows of Foley's at Christmastime.

Sometimes, Mother took me to the original James Coney Island for hot dogs in downtown Houston. I really loved it when we went to Woolworth's to eat lunch. They had the best dressing and gravy in the world, and my favorite dessert—german chocolate cake.

I wore beautiful clothes, and my mother bought me nice toys and expensive dolls that she carefully chose.

Mother chose my friends carefully too. Usually, they had to come to my house. Once, she allowed me to visit my science teacher's daughter at her house. Ruthann had a small, soft plastic doll that we were allowed to play with. We could brush her hair and change her clothes. When my mother came to pick me up, I told her I wanted a doll like Ruthann had.

We went to the toy store so I could show the doll to her. Mother took one look at it and adamantly refused to buy such a "cheap piece of plastic." I begged and tried to explain to her that it was an everyday doll, like my everyday clothes. I wouldn't have to take special care of her or worry about getting her dirty. I could play with the doll every single day and not worry about breaking it, unlike the hard plastic, movable head, arms, and legs dolls I had. She took great offense to that, accusing me of being unappreciative. She said, "You should take care of all your clothes and be grateful for your expensive toys."

I did. I was. Each one of them was named and dressed in fine evening gowns. They all looked perfect.

They still look perfect, and sit upon a high shelf in my home, along with their armoire full of doll clothes from the fifties era, each garment hung neatly on its own tiny hanger. A drop leaf, mahogany doll dining table with green-and-white-striped upholstered chairs, a high chair with Tiny Tears in her original outfit, a Bo-Peep baby bed, Tom Thumb cash register, and so many other toys join the old-new dolls on my shelf.

CHAPTER 3

Billy

I was six years old when my mother announced, "I've heard about a six-year-old boy who might be up for adoption."

An only child and lonely, I was overjoyed at the idea of having a brother my own age to talk to and spend time with. Most of my time was spent alone in my room reading, writing poetry, and listening to music. I loved doing all those things but thought it would have been more fun to share them with someone else.

It was a bright sunny day when we pulled up to the curb of a white, wood frame house, surrounded by a chain-link fence. My mother parked. She got out of the car, opened the gate, knocked on the door, and someone invited her in.

I saw a boy kneeling on the sidewalk, playing with a toy truck. He held the top of the truck with one hand and pretended to drive it, the way little boys do. I rolled down my window to get a better look. He had dark hair and deep brown eyes, the same color as mine. I wanted to talk to him, but he seemed so content that I didn't want to interrupt. He must have felt me watching him because he looked up and caught me staring. We both said, "Hi," at exactly the same time.

Still kneeling with one hand on the truck, he asked, "What's your name?"

I answered, "Vickie. What's yours?"

"Billy."

"Is that short for William?" *I like that name.*

"Yeah, I think so."

My brother's name will be William Faulkner, like the name on the books in our bookshelves. I smiled.

"I'm six. How old are you, Billy?"

"I'm six."

Mother came outside and introduced herself to Billy.

After a few minutes, a woman opened the door and called, "Billy!"

The boy stood up and asked, "Yes, ma'am?"

She said, "It's time to come inside."

Billy took his truck with him. I noticed his clothes as he shuffled inside. He wore a plaid shirt that was a little too small, jeans that were a little too short, and shoes that looked scuffed and worn out with their frayed and untied laces. He wasn't wearing socks. None of that mattered to me. Billy was the boy who might become my brother. And I was so proud of him.

Mother followed him inside the house. I got out of the car and sat on the porch step to wait. In a little while, my mother and Billy came out. She was carrying a paper sack. I thought it was probably Billy's treasures—the truck and whatever else was important to him.

I usually rode up front with Mother. That day, I wanted to sit in back with Billy. I wanted him to feel comfortable, and I knew if I sat in the front seat, I would keep turning around to look back at him. I guess Billy had just been given the news that he wouldn't be returning to his family. He was no longer friendly. He didn't want to talk. When we pulled away from the curb, he didn't look back toward the house, either. He sat on the front edge of the back seat, looked out his window, and never spoke a word. He didn't cry, but he looked sad. He didn't ask questions, but I knew he must have been confused. I'm sure he couldn't understand why or what was happening.

On the outside, he acted brave and strong. It made me hurt on the inside. I couldn't help but recall how devastating it was when I lost everything familiar to me. I remembered the pain of loss—the fear and the feelings of hopelessness and rejection. Tears filled my eyes. *I have to shake off those insecure feelings. I certainly don't want to be seen or heard. Mother might ask me what is wrong and she will be really upset if I tell her. I can never tell her the truth.* Protected by the blinding light of the evening sun and the glare it produced, I cried silently for him. He was already my brother in my heart. I couldn't have known it then, but this little boy—my brother, Billy—would someday protect me and save my sense of humor, my self-esteem, and my sanity.

It took a long time for Billy and me to get to sleep that first night. I was excited. There was no telling what tomorrow might bring. It was like the night before Christmas, Easter morning, and my birthday all rolled into one. Having a new brother to share everything with would make an ordinary day special.

Our rooms were next to each other, and it was late when I heard a sound coming from Billy's room—a sniffle and then more sniffling. At first, I thought he had a cold. Then I realized it was the sound of tears. I thought how easy it was in my happiness to forget the sadness of his loss. That night I was reminded to put myself in another's place, even when it was not a happy one. Then I heard "Now I lay me down to sleep; I pray the Lord my soul to keep." I joined in. "If I should die before I wake, I pray the Lord my soul to take. Amen." The near-silent sound of tears and words of a child's prayer echoed from each room.

Billy and I attended public school. He was in the first grade; I was in the second. Every day we waited for each other and walked home from school together. On occasion, we stopped along the way to pick blackberries growing through a neighbor's fence.

In elementary, we had school carnivals that served as fundraisers. Moms would meet at *our* house to do things like make hot dogs or fry doughnuts, to raise money for the PTA. We always knew when the PTA needed money. The smell of goodies coming from our house filled the air before we could run home and open the front door. When we did get home, we'd grab a snack then settle in for our favorite television show.

One show Billy and I never missed was *Kitirik*. She was a children's television character and a Channel 13 mascot from 1954 to 1971. The hostess was a young, pretty woman named Bunny Orsak. She dressed in a black cat outfit complete with ears, tail, and painted whiskers on her face.

There was only two months and one day between our ages. I was the oldest. Billy and I decided we would like to celebrate our next birthday on that TV show. We'd go together, pretending to be twins. We envisioned ourselves becoming rich as we reached into ole Nod the clown's "Wishing Well," filled with bright new pennies. Kitirik allowed birthday kids to scoop out a handful to take home with them. We couldn't imagine anyone giving away *that* much money. I'm sure Mother would have been happy to take us. She *loved* money, and there was the chance we could become little Bayou City stars. That is, until the day Kitirik interviewed one particular little birthday boy.

Billy and I were watching the show so intently that we didn't notice when Mother walked into the room. Kitirik asked the boy his name and how old he would be on his upcoming birthday. Like so many times before, she asked the boy if he had anything to say to "anyone out there in TV land." But this time, that turned out to be a *big* mistake. He replied, "Yes."

The boy had an ear-to-ear grin on his face. He lifted his right hand, as though to wave, then loudly and clearly stated, "Here's the *birdie* to you, Herbie!"

All emphasis was on the word *birdie* as he demonstrated the same with right hand, center finger. Our eyes and mouths dropped wide open. Billy and I immediately snapped our heads to look directly into each other's faces. Both sets of eyes were big as saucers. Had we actually heard what we thought we had? Things like that just didn't happen on live TV in 1954!

Our hopes of celebrating our next birthday, becoming wealthy, or ever appearing on KTRK's *Kitirik* were forever dashed when we saw our mother glaring at the television set where the 'Herbie hater' birthday kid had stood. We hoped she wouldn't ban the children's show. Just then, the channel went to a sudden, impromptu break. Now our job was to convince her that none of us had seen, or heard, what we thought we had.

That wasn't going to be easy. She was a woman on a mission. She had the telephone in one hand and a phone book in the other. She dialed, hung up; dialed, hung up; the line was busy for a long time. When she finally did get through, we heard her demand to speak with the president of the company.

"Me? I'll *tell* you who I am. I'm the president of the Parent-Teacher Association at Woodland Acres Elementary in the Galena Park Independent School District. Did you get all that?" She spoke very fast, and her voice rose with each word. I was sure whoever answered hadn't but was afraid to ask her to repeat it. I'll admit it sounded impressive.

"Yeah, Bob, what's going on over there at KTRK—putting that kind of trash out on a children's show? You'll have no kids watching from 'out *here* in TV land.' I can assure you of that. I'll get the entire school board involved if I have to. You, that cat, and clown will be looking for a new TV land to corrupt." She hung up and called the local newspaper.

She didn't ban *Kitirik* from our television. She decided it would be smarter to keep a "vigilant eye out for future infractions." Billy and I offered our help.

Unfortunately she would not allow us to celebrate our birthdays on the show. She said, "It wouldn't look right" after she had complained so forcefully. She added, "Besides, I don't want your names associated with any kind of show that promotes *deviant behavior.*"

Mother was very protective, and she was the ultimate *involved* Mom. She volunteered for everything but had one strict rule: "Never volunteer me for anything."

Her hospitality began and ended with things that centered on her children. She did whatever it took to promote and push us into the limelight. Mother couldn't be satisfied with status quo; we had to be the best at anything *she* chose for us to do. Surely she must have lived in a constant state of disappointment because things rarely—if ever—turned out that way.

With so much in common, and our constant struggle to try and please her, Billy and I became very close, exchanging secrets and feelings of inadequacy. It was a couple of years later when we learned how to become real blood brother and sister after watching an episode of *The Hardy Boys*. I was a little squeamish at the sight of blood, but he was *brave*, took the lead, and pricked his finger first. I followed, and we held our bleeding fingers together while making vows of eternal bond. From that day forward, we relentlessly supported one another.

Billy played Little League baseball and I went to every game, cheering for him and his team – appropriately named the Braves. He was athletic and made All Stars.

He was a Cub Scout, and I was a Brownie Scout. Mother became a den mother for each of us, helped me sell cookies, and hauled boys and girls to summer scout camps.

Mother strongly encouraged us to participate in school activities. She said, "Get your name out there, and broaden your horizons."

We weren't exactly sure what that meant. However, in time we became very familiar with the phrase and began to understand its meaning: Try lots of things, even if you look and feel like a fool doing it, and be sure everyone knows your (first) name. (If you succeed, you can tell them your last name.)

In the spring, sixth-graders, soon-to-be seventh-graders in junior high, were allowed to choose one of three electives: football, choir, or band. Billy was too small to play football and hated the thought of singing in the choir. He liked the look and sound of a cornet, so he decided to learn how to play. He joined the band.

Mother promptly went to the music store and purchased the shiny gold instrument, which was her golden ticket to an ulterior motive. The cornet wasn't enough for Mother. She insisted he become the drum major, the *leader* of the band.

Billy spent the entire summer after his sixth-grade school year taking private twirling lessons. He was forced to go to a contest where he won a trophy, partly because he twirled pretty well—if you didn't count all the drops and misses—but mostly because there were only a handful of boys who competed, not that there's anything wrong with it. I never saw the twirling trophy displayed with his baseball trophies.

Drum major tryouts were held late summer, and school started early fall. I don't remember if Billy ever learned to play a note on the cornet, but he looked real nice leading the school band. He never missed a beat, and the hat made him look a foot taller.

Her desire for me to shine among my peers didn't turn out as well. A particular experience stands out as having been one of the most, if not *the* most, embarrassing events of my life.

Unlike Billy, I could never be considered athletic. Regardless, at the end of my seventh-grade year, I competed for eighth-grade cheerleader. All the students and teachers gathered in the gymnasium to watch the tryouts and place their votes. My name was the first one called. Why couldn't my last name have started with a *Z*?

With black-and-gold pom-poms held high and shaking, I yelled, "Yea, yea ,... aa ... a," while running out onto a freshly waxed, highly polished and gleaming wooden stage floor. The new wax, ever so slick, made me slip in my nonskid tennis shoes. I got tangled up in my own legs, which caused me to trip. I didn't fall, but the trip itself made my stumbling feet and drunken legs lag behind. The upper part of my body was thrown forward, which caused it to move faster, thereby thrusting my head into an awkward, facedown position, looking more like a charging bull headed straight for the red drapes on the opposite side of the stage. Still, my legs and feet could not catch up. Momentum catapulted me across the stage. All the while, I was trying—nay, *praying*—to regain my balance. I ended up clinging to the draperies and having to reenter from the opposite side of the stage.

The gymnasium broke into uproarious laughter. Apparently, my performance had been hilarious. My face matched my red hair and the blood red drapes. Once the teachers, who were themselves laughing, got everyone settled down and under control, I was so embarrassed I couldn't think of one single clever comeback (e.g., custodian conspiracy). I almost forgot the cheer I was supposed to lead. That entire event did not work well for me, and I did not win a position on the squad. Who wanted Bozo the (redheaded) Clown for cheerleader? Later, at school, I laughed with the rest of them. At home, I cried.

Mother was not sympathetic when I described my disastrous, life-changing experience. She looked disgusted. She frowned, pursed her lips, shrugged, and let out a deep sigh. She said, "Sounds to me like you were acting silly."

What? Yes, Mother. I purposely humiliated myself and committed cheerleader suicide on stage at Woodland Acres Junior High…all for a laugh. Does my mother know me at all? Could she have the slightest idea who I was… am?

Mother's favorite word was *perseverance.* She made me promise to try again the following year, adding…"And I hope you will take it more seriously." I knew it would be a waste of time; it would take well over a year for everyone to forget the colossal calamity that had befallen me, changed my life, and stripped me of my pride. It might never be forgotten, but I had no pride left to lose, and the empty promise made her happy.

The activity Billy and I enjoyed most was roller skating. We were at Cook's Roller Rink every time the doors opened, except on Sunday. If we had not gone to church with our dad, he would not allow us to go skating. His rule made it easy for us to get our five-year Sunday school pins. That was the only say-so about us kids that Daddy ever had in that house. Otherwise, Mother didn't like or want his input. She had her own ideas and ways of handling situations and decisions regarding raising children. She would override any suggestions he might have. We learned early on who we answered to. If she chose to seek his help, that was fine, but he was not to interfere.

She didn't interfere with his idea of taking us to church on Sundays because she felt "children should be raised in church." She had lots of reasons why she didn't go. Sometimes, she had to stay home and rest so she could go watch us skate.

Once mother finally quit going to "watch us skate" (*spy on us*), Cook's became our refuge, a place of freedom from Mother's watchful eye. It was a place where it was safe to be ourselves—kids—and we could even act silly if we wanted to. Acting silly at home was not acceptable; acting silly in public was a violation—a rule breaker. Violations resulted in listening to hours of torturous lecture on the subject pertaining to whatever violation we had committed. Our mother was proficient in many areas, especially lecturing.

Billy loved to speed skate. He was first in line when Mr. Cook announced, "Time to line up for the boys' races." He usually won his age group. Sometimes the prize was free skating tickets. The girls thought he was cute and flocked to ask him to skate when the Ladies Choice overhead light lit up.

I was a good skater, and I met friends at the rink. Boys asked me to skate with them because I knew how. Sometimes, Mr. Cook would let me lead the Grand March. I really loved the loud music. My long red ponytail would fly as I would spin around, and I felt free as a bird.

CHAPTER 4

Jake (J. L.)

Three years after Billy came to live with us, one of Mother's good friends called to tell her about a nine-year-old boy, Jake. They called him J. L. He had been passed around from one foster home to another.

Mother hurried me into the car, and the two of us went to see him. He was the cutest little blond-headed boy with beautiful blue eyes. Before I even realized it, Mother had hurriedly placed Jake in the car to bring him home with us. If that sounds more like rescuing a stray and nothing like getting a brand new brother, that's because it was. I was very happy with the choice. But it seemed to me that Mother hadn't put much time or thought into her decision. I was afraid that in the long run my brother, J. L., would suffer for it. He did.

Mother didn't do him any favors by bringing him home that day. She had little to no patience with him. Someone told her, "J. L. has behavioral issues and a bad temper." I never knew who said that. I'm not sure why anyone would say such a hurtful thing about a child needing a home. Hadn't he been through enough? I believe that instead of relying on her own judgment, she allowed someone else's words to influence her, and she went with that preconceived opinion. That is why I don't think Mother gave him a fair chance. Maybe she considered him a challenge. It seemed like she was on constant guard, watching for him to misbehave or have a temper tantrum. She was always on the ready to "nip that in the bud before it starts." It's hard to be a fair and objective parent when you constantly expect the worst of a child. It's even harder to be the child whose parent always expects the worst.

J. L. hadn't had much guidance in life. It seemed to me that he just couldn't fit the mold fast enough.

Mother was always scolding him about something—slamming doors, talking too much, talking too loud, talking ... J. L. had a vivid imagination, but thinking out of the box was frowned upon. He was the square peg that Mother tried, unsuccessfully, to force into a round opening. Sometimes he argued that what he created in his mind was reality, or at the very least, "It could be." We might have been enjoying *Star Wars* years earlier, had his imagination and creativity not been stifled at such a young age. She said his "head was in the clouds," called him a "dreamer," and said he was "too headstrong."

When the two of them strongly disagreed, Mother requested that Daddy take charge of bringing him "back down to earth." Daddy's motto was "Spare the rod, and spoil the child."

Sometimes, Daddy would go to his locked closet and retrieve a razor strap. The race was on. You could hear him shout, "If you run, it will be twice as bad."

Given time, I guess its possible J. L. could have been *made* to reshape his rough edges and *made* to fit her idea of who he should be, what he should say, and what he should think. I'm not sure he could have ever conformed enough to Mother's liking.

J. L. didn't do well in school. In past times, he hadn't been forced to go, so he fell behind. However, he excelled in art. He was a natural. He loved to draw. You would have thought this could impress Mother since she was an excellent artist. It didn't. Billy could draw a horse's head, and Mother raved about it. That wasn't J. L.'s idea of "his type art." He preferred to sketch outer space and sci-fi. But he would—perhaps seeking kudos—draw the entire horse grazing in a beautiful green pasture with blue skies and cotton-candy clouds. It was just so-so.

Mother enjoyed making comparisons between us. Maybe competition through comparison was her (sick) idea of trying to bring out the best in each of us. The idea failed miserably and brought out the worst in her and the rest of us. It served as a means of pitting one child against the other. No wonder J. L. felt like nothing he did was ever good enough.

J. L. struggled through eleven grades of school and decided, with some subliminal encouragement, to join the navy. Pamphlets always lay around the house. On the covers were pictures of beautiful blue oceans and pretty girls in swimming suits. Inside was a picture of red-white-and-blue Uncle Sam, pointing and saying, "I Want You." J. L. took the bait. Mother signed to let him go at the age of seventeen, stating, "I think the discipline will be good for him."

We all knew the truth. She didn't know how to handle a kid who had a mind of his own. I missed him and loved it when he came home on leave. One time, he brought Mother an expensive gold pin with diamonds and matching earrings. He brought me a beautiful cameo ring, which I still have.

I really didn't understand my parents' issues with J. L. He was rebellious to so much control. He did speak his mind if he didn't agree with something said or done, but he was never a "bad kid." I don't think he felt as though he belonged, and I don't believe he ever felt loved. To this day, I think you could search the world over and never find anyone with a kinder, more compassionate heart.

When J. L. was discharged from the navy, he came home. He met and married a woman twenty years his senior. I think he was searching for something that sadly, he never found as a child.

Years later, J. L. was told, "You were never legally adopted." We were all surprised by the news, especially his wife. Since he had never been adopted, his last name was not Faulkner. That meant the names and signatures on their marriage license were invalid. I remember that for a while, they were both concerned as to whether the court acknowledged their marriage as legal. I'm not sure how they went about changing the name to his family birth name, but they did. Mother put her own spin to the story. She acted hurt when she said, "One day he just decided that he no longer wanted the last name of Faulkner."

CHAPTER 5

Evelyn

I never understood how Mother always seemed to know about families in need of help. But she did. I thought she might have a direct line to God—from her lips to His ears—or maybe she had a contact person, a mysterious angel-like informant who kept two lists: one list of those in need and another list of those who could fill the need.

The real mystery was that one day there would be some discussion about how nice it would be to have a brother or sister, and no sooner were the words spoken than Mother would hear of one. It was not only magical, it was timely.

I was almost ten-years-old when Mother and I agreed on how nice it would be to have a sister—two boys and two girls, a perfect family. About that same time, she heard of a family living in Houston in dire need of help. The mother was trying to raise several children, mostly on her own. The father was rarely there. Mother said, "He probably came home just long enough to get the woman pregnant, and then he would be gone again."

She discovered that the family was living in an apartment building off San Felipe in an undesirable part of town. That did not deter Mother. One afternoon, she and I set out to find them.

Several people were hanging out around the complex. A few were standing in front of doors or leaning on the railings. Others were talking in small groups. They stopped what they were doing and began to watch us. I remember being a little uncomfortable, feeling out-of-place, as we climbed up the stairs to the small apartment. Mother knocked, and a woman came to the door. She was thin and frail-looking, which made her appear older than Mother thought she was. She looked as tired and worn out as the long faded dress and the gray sweater she was wearing. The lady had no expression—neither one of surprise nor that she expected us. Her lack of expression made me wonder if Mother had talked to her before we got there that evening. She opened the door and invited us in.

The room was dimly lit, but I could see several children. Mother talked to the woman for a long time, but I couldn't hear what they were saying. Later, I was introduced to a girl named Evelyn, and a boy, one of her brothers. I think she called him Sonny. Evelyn and Sonny got their belongings, and shortly after that, the four of us left. The trip home was quiet. By the time we arrived, it was dark outside. Mother turned into the three-car driveway and honked the horn. The outside lights came on and J. L. emerged from the house. He walked across the lawn and opened the garage door for us.

Once we got inside and introductions were made, Mother called her friend Phyllis. I overheard her say that we were back at home, and she could come over. Phyllis lived very close and was there in just a few minutes. She took Sonny to her house, and Evelyn stayed with us. Later, I heard that things didn't work out for him with Phyllis, so he was returned to his mother.

Although Evelyn wasn't nearly the oldest of ten children in her biological family—her age placed her in the middle—she was the nurturing type. One year, Mother sent us to a private school. There was no cafeteria available. Every morning, Evelyn would get up early, make sandwiches, and pack a lunch for each of us. I guessed she had been used to helping out with her siblings.

I often wondered about her memories of those brothers and sisters. I would imagine she missed them very much, but if she did, she never talked about it.

Evelyn was a quiet person. She didn't share much information about anything. It seemed like she chose to keep the line of communication to a minimum. Getting to know someone is very difficult when that person chooses not to let you in. It was frustrating for me. I thought it might be personal—her own self-protection mechanism.

It was hard to figure out whether Evelyn was happy with her transition to our family. We shared a room, and it wasn't long before additional closet space had to be added. I know she was happy with all the new clothes.

That fall when school started, she fit right in with all the kids. She was very pretty with her blonde hair and blue eyes. She was well liked. In fact, she was popular. In the ninth grade, she was voted cheerleader. That same year, she won homecoming queen. She had a few close friends, but back then, I never felt I was one of them.

Evelyn was twelve years old when she came to live with us. It took her a long time to adjust to calling Mother by any name. That made Mother angry. One time, she told Evelyn, in a loud voice, "When you talk to me, address me as Alma or Mother, something, *anything* to let me know you are addressing me."

After more than twelve years, calling a different woman Mother had to be quite an adjustment. Maybe that was the reason I didn't think she considered me a sister. The relationship between the two of us was strained. I felt she was either embarrassed by me— understandable, I guess, with red hair, braces on my teeth, the Bozo cheerleader tryout incident (which does have a tendency to follow you)—or she just didn't like me. Trying to figure it out was exasperating.

There was definitely some sibling rivalry between the two of us. I began to think she felt Mother was partial to me. Maybe she thought it was because I had been there for so long, and she was the newcomer. I decided that had to be it. She was older but newer. It all began to make more sense.

That scenario could really screw up the pecking order theory. However, that thought was a far cry better then thinking she was embarrassed by me, or she didn't like me. I settled on that reasoning. In any case, she may have been right about the partiality, in the beginning. But things changed as time went on.

I am happy to say that over the years, I got my braces off—my teeth were straight—my hair went from bright red to dark auburn, and Evelyn and I have grown close. We are more like sisters now than ever before.

We are able to laugh about things from our childhood, things that once hurt our feelings or made Billy and me envious. At one time, Billy and I were the only two children in the house, but when Evelyn came, she was the only one allowed to trim the Christmas tree. Mother said it was because "she had so much talent and a gift for decorating." Billy and I gave her the title Miss Decorator. She would get mad and threaten to tell on us when we wouldn't let up on the name-calling.

I didn't inherit any of Mother's artistic ability or her flair for design and sewing. However, Evelyn—with all her *decorating skills*—demonstrated aptitude and talent in each category with special emphasis on the art of cornice board design, manufacturing, and refurbishing. We had lots of windows in our room, which provided an ample practice field. By the time Evelyn was old enough to work with such dangerous heavy equipment as the sewing machine, (which totally impressed Mother) the steel foot pedal was beginning to be replaced by knee control. That would eventually prove to be a much safer design for all, especially for Billy and me.

Our sister had previously declared us a couple of "brats" who loved to aggravate her. Therefore, on occasion, we felt obligated to come up with a plan that would be worthy of the title *she* had so generously bestowed upon *us*.

She was seated at the sewing machine, prepared to make—yet another set of—new (clap!), improved (clap-clap!) cornice boards to impress Mother. Billy had hidden under the yards of material piled on the floor and was ready to tickle her leg with scratchy broom straws. I stood next to her, feigning interest in the project. I said, "That's gonna' look "swell"—code word, *'swell'*—I screamed, 'Flying Roach' then I counted, '1-Mississippi, 2-Mississippi.' Billy scratched her leg with the 'straw roach legs' and the plan was set in motion. The next thing we knew, she was screaming and pressing the *foot* pedal toward the floor, smashing his hands and fingers, while kicking at him with her other foot and slapping at me. We knew beforehand that we would get a strong reaction, but we both agreed that any injury incurred was worth watching the yards of material fly, causing a rip-out and redo. That was just the price she had to pay for being so 'talented.' We hadn't considered the hefty price we would pay due to Mother's wrath.

Still, laughter can quickly become tears when some little thing said—a song on the radio, a movie—can ignite the emotions of one or both of us. I recall the sad feelings left behind in me after I watched the 1991 movie *A Thousand Acres*. It is a realistic story dealing with loyalty, innocence, child abuse, pitting one against another, and, finally, betrayal. The story evoked feelings in me that persist to this day. When I returned home from the theater, I called Evelyn and insisted she go see it. I needed someone to share all that hurt and grief. It doesn't matter whether a memory is hilariously funny or excruciatingly painful; both prove to be beneficial when we share our thoughts and feelings. But whoever said "Laughter is the best medicine" is brilliant.

Evelyn and I have discovered a way to recycle pain and tears. We can say that our emotions have "gone green." Here's how the five-step transformation program works:

Step 1)	Recall:	One of us recalls an incident.
Step 2)	Share:	We share it with the other.
Step 3)	Confide:	We confide in one another. (We can; we both came from the same *Funny Farm*.)
Step 4)	Realize:	We realize whatever created inner turmoil and strife,
Step 5)	Let Go:	We are now able to let go. Tears become laughter.

My sister and I don't get together nearly enough, but recently we were on a short road trip. I call those little trips "healing time." Getting away from our daily routine helps both of us. What benefits us most is sharing stories and feelings we were never allowed to have or talk about as kids. She recently told me a story. Her words touched my heart and brought tears to my eyes.

She said, "Before I came to live with y'all at Mama's house, a man and woman took me to live with them. When we arrived at their house, I saw all the pretty clothes bought for me. The clothes were neatly placed on my new bed. There were blouses and crop tops, cute Bermuda shorts, pedal pushers, and long pants—everything you could imagine. And then I saw it! It was the most beautiful yellow dress I had ever seen. You *know* how much I love yellow!"

Evelyn told me that the man and woman argued all night long. She said, "I heard screaming and things being thrown. It scared me. I didn't want to stay there. It made me feel uncomfortable to see them the next morning. That's when I told both of them that I wanted to go back home to my mother."

The woman told me, "We'll take you back, but you will *not* be allowed to take any of the new clothes with you."

"I said, 'That's okay.' But I just couldn't leave that yellow dress behind. I stuffed it in my bag and hid it beneath my old worn-out and faded things. I took that yellow dress back home with me."

I was very proud of her. I never thought my
sister would have had that much guts.

CHAPTER 6

Mom and Dad

Mother was the single surviving child of three. There had been two other children—twins, a boy and a girl. They died of diphtheria before their first birthday. It was understandable that two parents who suffered such great loss and tragedy would spoil their only surviving child. Unfortunately, they reared a selfish little girl who always got her way.

She was extremely proud of the fact that she had graduated from business-college back in the day when girls rarely thought about going to college, even if they could afford it. Mother's parents were certainly not wealthy, but they sacrificed to give their daughter more than most children had back then. Mother was educated, self-confident, independent, and business-minded (*I love these qualities*) with a strong, overbearing, and controlling personality (*not so much*).

Her life had not been typical for a child born of that generation (early 1900s), and she did not grow up to be your typical southern woman. She didn't like to cook or clean and preferred yard work to domestic duties. People always commented on the beautiful roses she grew. She didn't have to try. She had a green thumb. It seemed all she had to do was stick a plant in the ground, give it a little water, stand back, and watch it grow. There was no rhyme or reason to her gardening. If she saw an empty space, it became a picturesque and fragrant bed of roses.

She was a very talented artist and sold much of her work at art shows. I remember when someone once commented, "I can't understand how Alma paints such beautiful, delicate pictures with her large hands."

Those hands didn't just create beautiful works of art; she was an excellent seamstress. Mother didn't need a pattern. Sometimes, she took Evelyn and me to expensive downtown boutiques where she found designer, one-of-a-kind, girly dresses to sketch. Then she'd go home, drag out the ole (pedal to the metal) Singer, and—*bippety, boppety, boo*—there they were, looking exactly like the ones we had seen in the high-priced stores. One day, a clerk saw what she was doing and told her to take the sketchpad, us, and leave. That didn't bother her one bit.

Evelyn and I were a little embarrassed. We didn't act like it. We still wanted her to make the dresses. But we had never been kicked out of a store before. Mother said the lady was jealous and probably made peanuts for money. When I think about it, I wonder why we didn't carry our Brownie Hawkeye's and take snapshots of the clothes.

Mother was a tall, big-boned woman with broad shoulders and a large frame. She told us she played basketball in college and was a good player until she got hurt in a game. She said that was the reason she couldn't have children. I had no idea women played basketball that long ago. Having seen pictures of swimsuits from that era, I couldn't help but wonder what their uniforms looked like. I don't really know the extent of her college injury. She tried to elaborate, but when she used the word *womb*, my ears stopped working. I believed she was afraid of childbirth and didn't like sex. She scowled and winced at both subjects.

Mother was self-employed. She owned several rental properties located on lots next to and near our house. She told us girls how important it was to do business with someone who treated a woman as an equal. She boasted that the president of the Galena Park Bank told her, "Mrs. Faulkner, if you ever need a loan for a business venture, just come to see me."

Mother and Daddy kept all their money separate. Each had their own account and checkbook. One time, I asked her why.

She told me a story about how right after they were married; she bought a pair of shoes and some expensive clips to go on them. When she brought the packages home, Daddy saw the receipt, and they argued over the price. She wasn't about to let any *man* tell her what to do with *her* money. From that day forward, finances were kept separate. As time went on, other things were kept separate, such as bedrooms.

When it became acceptable for women to wear pants, she abandoned her nice dresses and didn't pay much attention to her appearance or what others thought of her. The only people she cared to impress were wealthy, and they were almost always men. She said, "Most women are dull and boring, and I have nothing in common with them."

I'm sure it never crossed her mind that they might feel the same way about her.

I remember a time when Mother surrounded herself with lady friends. In fact, I believed it was the reason she built those homes. She was in complete control of who lived nearby. She only rented to friends or to people whom she thought could be "acceptable" friends. Most of those old friends moved on to become homeowners themselves, I think that's when she began to lose interest in the property. By that time, we kids had flown the coop, and she didn't have her helpers at home anymore. She had to hire someone. All of us went back from time to time to give her a hand. She had a way of guilting each of us into that. Maybe she lost interest because the homes were getting older, and so was she.

Mother quit investing any money on repairs and focused on how much more she might be able to collect. She let her rent property run down, but the amount of rent she collected never did follow suit. It remained the same or continued to increase. Poor people (like many of her renters) didn't seem to matter, unless she needed them for a particular purpose.

Maria was a small child when her parents rented a house from Mother. She spoke fluent English and Spanish and served as an interpreter between Mother and her Hispanic renters. This placed the shy young child in an extremely awkward position. Mother didn't know what Maria might be saying, and half the time, poor little Maria didn't understand what the words she had been told to say meant. Mother, in her intimidating way, towered over her, arms folded, and with a sour expression on her face, sternly stated, "I want you to tell them exactly what I said. I don't care if they like it or not. They can just move!"

Maria tried to tell them, but if Mother didn't think she was getting the point across fast enough, or with enough passion in her voice, she endeavored to demonstrate her disapproval of their dastardly deed, by acting out or pantomiming. Together, they reminded me of the old two-man comedy act Laurel and Hardy. The Double M performances (Mother and Maria) drew a crowd of inquisitive children. They watched Mother as she pretended to pour grease down an already clogged drain. Meanwhile, Maria would be looking at them and with her shaming index finger moving from side to side, she would say, "No! No!" Sometimes, Mother would mow a make-believe overgrown lawn with an imaginary lawn mower. That resulted in "*corte la llarda*" ('cut the yard,' in Spanglish) from Maria. The whole show looked and sounded like good cop, bad cop. It was hard for anyone to take six-year-old Maria seriously or, for that matter, Mother the Mime. Kids would emulate her right down to the sound of the lawn mower. A few had their own plastic toy mowers. They would grab them and form their own kind of conga dance line behind her. Maria had to tell adults, "Next time you are late paying rent, the drain gets stopped up, or the lawn needs mowing, (whatever the offense might be) you will be held responsible to pay the bill or move." This was not an easy task for the little girl. Sometimes, renters got mad at her—and she had to go to school with their children.

Daddy owned an auto parts store on Market Street. He began his business during the Depression years. Realizing there was a shortage of tires, he gathered used ones, and progressed from there. He told us stories about those lean and hungry years. He was the oldest of thirteen children and earned pennies a day by making soup and serving it to those in line for stamps and food. That is probably the reason why our pantry was always full. If pork and beans were on sale; we might have five cases in the pantry; the same with corn and other canned goods. Daddy never wanted to be without food again.

Mother was frugal, but Daddy made her look like a big spender. When we were in elementary, lunches cost $1.25 a week. Daddy would wrap the quarter tightly with a one-dollar bill and leave four, wrinkle-free, quarter-sized squares on the kitchen table. I thought the reason he did that was so he could spend a little more time with his money. On Monday mornings, we kids would take one square each to buy our lunch for the week. Daddy followed that procedure all the way through our senior year, when lunches were at least that much daily. Mother made up the difference until we got part-time jobs. Still, Daddy used to say, "Alma is so tight that she could squeeze a nickel till the buffalo's eyes bulged out."

If any of us found a stray nickel, Daddy would demand to see it. He held it up close to a light and thoroughly examined it for *bulging eyes* before he decided whether we could claim it. I couldn't help laughing, but those words could start an argument right away, over who was the tightest. Daddy had (what I called) 'argument advantage' because he wore a hearing aid. I'd see him reach between the buttons on his shirt to turn the volume down. Mother and Daddy argued regularly about one thing or the other. Many times, Daddy retreated to his car to sleep. No wonder Daddy went to the store before daybreak and didn't come home until after dark.

Except for the homemade, hand-churned kind, (using electricity would have been a waste) we never tasted real ice cream until we left home. Daddy told us, "Mellorine is so much better." That was like saying lard was better than butter. One time, after he cranked the ice cream maker for what seemed like hours, he told us to bring our bowls. Mother was first in line. Daddy scooped a portion into her bowl. She told him to put *more* in the bowl. He did. Once again, she waved her hand toward the dish and said, "a little more." After the third time, he said, "Don't you think that's enough? The bowl needs sideboards on it now!"

I am a very visually imaginative person, and his words struck me as so funny that I laughed until I cried. Mother glared at me, stormed off into the house, and slammed the door behind. Her mountain of ice cream made it, unscathed.

Daddy had rigid standards. He hated a liar and often said, "If a person will lie, he will steal."

He told us a story about a man who came into his store. The man purchased a Coke (six cents) from the Coke machine. He began to look around in the display cases. He opened the heavy glass front door to leave. Just then, Daddy hurled an empty bottle at him, which struck him in the back. He turned to ask, "Why?"

"You're stealing that!" Daddy responded.

"I paid for this," the man replied as he raised the bottled drink.

Daddy said, "You're a liar! You paid for the Coke, but there's a two-cent deposit on the bottle!"

There were a couple of generation gaps between our parents and us. While that made life harder during our growing up years, I think it served us well as adults. We learned responsibility at an early age, and we all have excellent work ethics. We never expected anyone to give us something for nothing. Mother reinforced that idea by charging interest on any money we borrowed from her, another lesson well learned. Thanks, Mom.

CHAPTER 7

The Visit

It was June, 1958. School was finally out. I was almost ten and looking forward to a carefree summer. I was awakened by an early-morning knock on the door. The doorbell rang, and the knocks became louder. I heard the door open, and my mother's voice. She was talking to a man. I closed my eyes and tried to get back to sleep. Suddenly, I heard someone running up the stairs. I knew it was one of the kids, and it must be something important. Whoever it was began to leap up the steps, taking two and three at a time. It was my sister Evelyn. She said, "Get dressed, and come downstairs!"

When she said that, my eyes flew wide open. I stared straight ahead and didn't move. *What have I done this time?*

I could almost feel my semi lifeless brain switch gears. The process of cerebral resurrection began with what felt like a sudden jolt that threw the brain into reverse; there was a brief pause, then a high-pitched, high-speed rewind. When the answer was recovered, it would trigger an automatic playback from the memory bank. I waited ... nothing—completely silent.

"What's wrong? What did I do?" I asked my sister, anxiously.

"Nothing, you didn't do anything. Your mother and brothers are here to visit," she replied, excited.

"Oh, okay." I breathed a sigh of relief.

All of a sudden, her words hit me like a freight train hauling asphalt!

I was dazed and confused by a total lack of understanding about what I had just heard and what was going on. I threw the cover back, got out of bed, and stumbled toward the light shining through my bedroom window. I formed an L-shape with my hand and placed it above my eyes. I tried squinting, but that was more about bringing an inconceivable picture into focus than anything at all to do with the sun. A strange car had parked in the driveway. Sitting inside the car was a woman, a man, and two boys. Another man, who I didn't know, walked from our front door to the car. He stopped and talked to the woman through the open window on the passenger side.

I felt someone staring at me. I turned my head and saw Mother standing in my doorway. The look on her face told me she was upset. Mother said, "You don't have to see them unless you want to."

Then I was really confused. It sounded as if I was being offered a choice—to see them or not. Evelyn told me who they were, but Mother always taught me to be afraid of "them." She had warned me many times, "If you're walking home from school and strangers approach you, even if they know your name and where you live, it could be "those people." She told me I should run home as fast as I could, and not say a word. "They will grab you, and you will never see me again." She made it very clear.

Needless to say, I was a little fearful of them. But I was almost ten years old and had the curiosity of a ten-year-old child. I wanted to see my brothers. I barely remembered them. I wanted to see my real mother. I didn't remember her at all.

I did know what she looked like. One time she sent me a big teddy bear and a picture of herself. It was a picture in a lime green frame of a beautiful woman with short dark hair and brown eyes. She was wearing a black dress that came down on both shoulders. She had on a white pearl necklace and pearl earrings. I quickly memorized every single detail. I must have looked longer than I thought, because after what seemed like a few seconds, my mother took it away. I was allowed to keep the bear.

One day when I was trying to find something in Mother's drawer, I ran across the picture by accident. Another time, I purposely slipped it out of its hiding place to show my best friend, Carol, who agreed the lady was beautiful. I told Carol, "She is my birth mother; her name is Gloria, and she always sends me birthday and Christmas cards, but I never get to keep them."

I had no memory of ever having seen her "in real life." So, yes, I was curious about this mystery woman, and I did want to meet her, but I had to be careful.

I believe it was at that moment when I first realized the value of hiding my feelings. Mother was asking a question and making a profound statement. "You don't have to see them unless you want to."

I had fallen prey to that kind of loaded comment before. If I said no, she would use it as an excuse to send them all on their way. If I said yes, she would probably be angry with me, as though this surprise visit was something that I, a ten-year-old child, may have conjured up. She might act hurt, and maybe she would be. I couldn't take any chances, not with something this big, this important. I didn't want to hurt anyone's feelings, least of all my mother's. I guess that statement could be confusing, sort of like "Who's on first?" My mother has always been my adopted mother, and my birth mother is Gloria.

Mother was still standing in the doorway. I knew she was waiting for me to say I didn't want to see them. Instead, I asked, "Where did they come from?"

She replied, "Michigan."

I said, "That seems like a long way. I think we should at least say hello to the boys, don't you? After all, they're just kids."

Who could say no to kids? I was pleased with the outcome of my first diplomatic manipulation. However, after that day, I don't think diplomacy ever worked for me again, not with Mother, anyway. I know manipulation never did.

I remember how fast the day flew by. Pictures were taken of me with Mother and Daddy, me with the twins, Jim and Harold, and me with my birth mother, Gloria, and her husband, Dale. Mother insisted that my sister, Evelyn, be in almost every picture. I think it was to make sure anyone who might see them would know I belonged to another family.

Gloria loved my auburn hair. It was long, hanging past my hips. They were getting ready to leave when she asked if she could cut a lock of my hair for a "keepsake." I looked at my mother. No one was allowed to touch my hair without her permission. She went to get the scissors. Just as Gloria started to cut, my mother's warnings popped into my head. I flinched and asked her, "Are you going to stab me?"

She said, "No, I could never hurt you; you are my little girl."

"Do you have any other little girls?" I asked.

"No, you're my only one."

I don't know if it was the words, the way she said them, or the way she looked at me that made me feel so special. At that moment, I secretly wished she would ask me to go home with her, but she didn't. I wouldn't have; I couldn't have. I just needed to know that she wanted me.

What stands out most in my memory of their visit and about that day is something intangible. It is a feeling—a deep, unfulfilled yearning in my heart. It was truly, as they say, a burning desire. My longing was for the two of us, Gloria and me, to have been allowed a little time together to talk, alone. We weren't able to say the things that needed saying. We couldn't ask questions that needed answering.

We hadn't been able to hug one another in the way I needed hugging; the loving and protective way a mother hugs her child. Had she needed those things too? How would I ever know?

When the car pulled away, the emptiness I felt left a hole in my heart. We hadn't been allowed to share any emotion. She had been so close and real yet so far and inanimate. I felt like a little girl who had just lost her birthday balloon, a beautiful pink one with a smiley face, filled with helium so it could rise above all obstacles. I loved that balloon, and I felt a very real connection to it. Suddenly, the string slipped from my small hand. Try as I might, I couldn't get it back. I wanted it back. I needed it. I knew that I would never hold it again. It kept drifting farther and farther away. The only thing left for me to do was cry, but that was not allowed. I had to cry silently and never let anyone see. I began to wonder: Would I ever see it again, the beautiful pink one with a smiley face? And if I did, would it be too late? Would I have outgrown the desire that left me wanting and needing so much more?

That night I wanted to talk about the events of the day. I went to Billy's room and lay down across his bed. He was quiet, so I asked him what was wrong. He didn't say a word. I asked, "Are you upset because my family came to see me?"

He replied, "No."

Anxiously, I asked him three questions at one time. I wanted to know right away, what was bothering him? I needed to make it right.

"Then what's wrong? Didn't you have fun with the boys? Didn't you like them?"

"Yes."

Silence again. I thought about it for a while and finally asked, "Is it because you miss your family and wish they would come to see you?"

There was no answer. He turned on his side so I couldn't see his face, but I could hear his tears, so I knew. I wished I could have thought of something to say, something that would make him feel better, but all I could do was lie down by his side and put one arm around him.

The next day, Mother asked, "Did the visit bother you?" *Warning! Proceed with caution!*

I answered, "It was really good to see the boys. I thought Gloria and Dale were nice." *Slow down.*

My answer was not what she wanted.

She said, "I think those boys were out of control. They slammed doors, ran in and out of the house, and yelled like heathens when they were in the yard." The whole conversation was about to take a turn for the worse. *Danger! Sharp turn ahead!*

She added, "They acted like the wild men from Borneo."

I was just about to ask her who those men were when she continued with her rant.

"And you think Gloria is so nice? You know she had another child she gave away." *Curve!*

I wondered if Gloria had lied about me being "[her] only little girl." The words had meant a lot to me.

"Boy or girl?" I quickly responded.

She answered without hesitation. "A boy."

I couldn't have known any of that, and I didn't need or want to hear it. After I thought about it for a minute, I wondered if Mother was making it up to make me dislike Gloria.

I asked, "How do you know? Who told you?"

"She did! She wrote me a letter and told me all about it. I still have the letter around here somewhere. I'll show it to you."

I wanted to see the letter, but Mother never did show it to me. The subject was completely dropped. I wondered about the letter's existence. But if what she said was true, I had another brother out there somewhere. I guess I wasn't smart enough (or dumb enough) to have asked why Gloria would have shared that very private information with her, but over the years, I think the answer has indirectly surfaced.

Mother and Daddy made a trip to Tennessee when I was about five years old. I was left at home with Grandma and Unckie (nickname for my uncle). They went to visit Gloria, who was attending nursing school at the time. They asked her to sign adoption papers. She was reluctant to do so but knew she had nothing to offer a child.

Years later, Gloria told me, "Mr. Faulkner got down on his knees and begged me to sign the papers, and Mrs. Faulkner promised to treat me as though I was her daughter. She told me, 'It will be like we are adopting two girls and you can come to Houston to visit anytime.' Gloria said, 'I trusted her.'

While Gloria and I never once discussed whether she gave birth to another son, I believed that if there was such a letter, she wrote it because she "trusted" Mother to keep her secret. I decided to honor that trust, even though my mother hadn't.

I found out that the other man who came with them to visit that day was my uncle J. B., another one of my birth father's brothers. J. B. lived in Pearland, Texas. I didn't know that back then. I learned that when J. B. came to the door on Gloria's behalf, Mother told him, "No, they cannot come in."

Supposedly, he said some magic words that changed her mind. Those words continue to be a mystery to me.

Not long after that, both the teddy bear and the picture disappeared. I looked for them many times but never saw them again. A few years later, my brother, J. L., told me, "After the visit, Mother made me take the picture and the bear out to the railroad trestle and toss them into Greens Bayou, the water below." I visualized the episode; first the teddy bear landed with a loud splash, sending the dirty brown water rippling out into semicircles. Just as my brother was about to release the picture, a sudden gust of wind almost carried it to safety at the shore's edge. All at once, everything became still, even the surrounding trees. The picture hesitated, giving me a final look. Then it floated down and landed on top of the water. It stayed afloat for a second, and I could see her smile just below the water. Then it began to drift farther away, just like the balloon had those years earlier, when I was ten. Again, I felt the emptiness that had once left a hole in my heart.

I couldn't have known it then, but that visit, in the summer of 1958, was the last time I would ever see my brother, Jim.

Harold

Jim

CHAPTER 8

Growing Up

Things changed for us again as we became a little older. Life was no longer all fun and games. Work was not optional. Weekends would find Evelyn and me busy painting, cleaning, and patching rent houses that had become vacant. We scrubbed filthy floors and toilets, and washed, ironed, and hung fresh curtains. We did whatever it took to help Mother prepare homes for the next renters. When there were no vacancies, we worked at home waxing furniture, vacuuming, and cleaning the living room. We did not do those things for money but so we could go out with friends or invite them over on Friday or Saturday night. We had to earn that right.

In much the same way, we had to earn Mother's love. It was not given freely. She needed to be proud of us through good grades, acknowledgments, talents, or deeds. If we made a B she couldn't understand why we hadn't put forth a little more effort to make A's. Things always seemed to fall a little short of being "good enough."

One day, I was sitting on the sofa in our living room, crying. I had just been notified by mail (and received my white ribbon trimmed in gold lettering) that I won third place in a writing contest. There had been lots of participants, since it had been a state tournament. I was told to fill in at the last moment when the chosen student became ill. Prior to that, I had never entered anything except debate, prose reading, or duet acting. I was receiving the news of my win, via mail, almost a week after the contest. Mother seemed proud. She told me I did a good job. "*But*, next time, you should be able to win first."

I sat there crying. I not only had let her down, l had let me down. I asked, "Why can't I ever be the *best* at something?"

Mother's response was, "Third isn't bad; you'll just have to work harder."

Once I got past the self-pity session, sorted things out, and began to think clearly, I realized the loss (yes, loss—the glass was half-empty, not half-full) had actually taught me something very valuable. I had stressed, worried, and almost wasted the entire day thinking about what improvements I might have made. The tournament representatives mailed me a copy of the paper I wrote, along with the third-place ribbon. I read it a couple of times and thought about the overall effect this silly contest had on me. The truth was, the paper was pretty good. I doubted I would have changed one thing, even if I had known the outcome of the contest. The words I wrote expressed my own personal opinion. There had been no right or wrong answer.

There were three topics to choose from. I happened to select "Should extracurricular activities of teens be limited to weekends?" The premise of my answer was based on whether the teen could handle the responsibility of extra activities during the week along with his or her school work and any other mandatory duties. I wrote the best paper I could. I wouldn't have said anything different whether the judge(s) agreed or not. I realized that I might never be able to win in that "Ready Writing" event, certainly not if the judge(s) disagreed with my opinion. Maybe I selected the wrong topic. Maybe my selection had been a subject that bored them to death. Regardless, I decided the desire to be first should never overpower a person's true opinion. It should never influence individuals to compromise themselves or their beliefs. (Obviously, presidential elections excluded.) *Besides, isn't first a temporary thing? What if I had won first? That didn't mean I always would or could.* Instead of Judge Roy Bean, I might end up with Judge Judy.

Nothing stays the same. While we should always strive to do our best, there will always be someone who can do better, someone who will outdo another—whether in writing, acting, piano, cheerleading, whatever it might be. In the same way, there's always someone with better clothes, a nicer house, car, etc. Coming to grips with all that was a huge help for me. It reduced my stress level. It also reduced the amount of pressure I put on myself. For a little while, I quit chewing my fingernails, and they began to grow. But that was only temporary.

The event inspired a noticeable change in me and my attitude. Mother seemed a bit bewildered and concerned. She didn't know how to deal with the fact that I was growing up—beginning to develop a mind of my own. I no longer had a need for a puppeteer to manipulate my every thought and action.

After the mail was delivered, along with all the drama it brought, Evelyn and I resumed our inside chores. I guess Billy and J. L. must have been raking leaves and mowing the lawn. It always seemed to look nice, and Daddy was at work before daylight, where he stayed until way after dark. He worked every day except Sunday, when we went to church. Sometimes he couldn't help but nod off during a sermon. One of us would nudge him, and he would whisper, "I'm not asleep; I'm just resting my eyes."

Since Daddy didn't hear well, his whispers were louder than he thought. I'm sure lots of the congregation knew when he needed to 'rest his eyes.' In my life, I have had several occasions to recall and quote those words.

Our grandmother did all the cooking until she was no longer able. Evelyn and I washed, dried, and put the dishes away. Grandma and our uncle (Unckie) lived with us. There were eight people in the thirty-five-hundred-square-feet house. Growing up, we never thought the house was big. We never thought about it one way or the other. I guess it didn't seem big because there were so many people to fill it. Looking back, I realize it was large in comparison to our friends' homes.

We did, however, realize our yard was big. Evelyn and I often had football parties after our Woodland Acres Friday-night junior high games. We made trays of sandwiches, and Daddy brought home cases of little bottled Cokes and Dr. Peppers from his store. That was lots of fun and those times remain etched in our memories, as well as the memories of many of our friends from back then.

It was 1962 when once again, I swallowed my pride, fulfilled Mother's request to "persevere," and tried out for ninth-grade cheerleader. By then, I had overcome some of my clumsiness. That time, without any type of grand entrance, I made it. However, it did not turn out to be a good thing.

My mother, who apparently felt like cheerleading was a real job to be taken seriously and handled with professionalism, sat in the football stands making spastic gestures at me. She got my attention by flapping her arms up and down. Then, in contrast, she quickly assumed a grandeur-like posture, shoulders flung back and head tilted up. She over-exaggerated the action so much that I couldn't figure out the message she was trying to convey. It looked to me like some sort of fish-swallowing pelican. I wished the ground in front of the pep squad would open up and swallow *me*. I mastered the owl-like art of looking around without turning my head, to see if anyone was watching. She would often place her index fingers at the edges of her mouth and draw an exaggerated invisible upward line on both sides of her face. In my mind's eye, all I could see was a set of huge red clown lips staring at me from the bleachers. I thought it was another mime performance, but I finally caught on. She was reminding me to stand up straight with my head held *high* and *smile*! If I huddled with the other cheerleaders, and we laughed, she would glare at me with a disgusted look on her face. That meant I would get a lecture all the way home on acting silly. I can barely recall pep rallies, Friday-night-lights or leading cheers. This 'job' was obviously not supposed to be fun. I certainly don't remember it that way.

By the time we got to high school and began to have close friends and boyfriends, things changed again. Mother was in her sixties, and she went a little crazy.

Big hair was in. We had to get up early to get ready for school. I don't think we had an alarm clock in our room. We didn't need one. I often wondered if Mother went to bed or if she nested on the stairway. Every morning, there she was like a trained rooster perched on the banister at the foot of the stairs, crowing up at us before the break of day. In the harshest, shrillest, humanly impossible pitch, she squawked, "Vick-eeeee, Vick-eeeee." The *eeeee's* soared up the scale, leaped over octaves, and took on an all-new frequency, rivaling that of a fire engine siren. I wanted to go back to sleep but tried to respond quickly, "I'm up!" I hated it when the neighbor's dogs started howling.

I teased my hair on top, combed it down, and lifted it back up—over and over. To my delight, the repetitious action removed all signs of natural wave and curl. It somehow straightened and stretched each strand which now seemed to stand at attention, making the hair appear longer and taller than it really was. No doubt that is how the beehive was created. When I felt my hair was presentable for my peers, I went downstairs to leave.

Mother was waiting for me on the first step. She gave a non-verbal warning look that spoke loud and clear. It silently screamed in a deep, dark Vader-voice—Do Not Move!

When she returned, the 'warning look' had significantly changed into something of sheer horror. It had become a terrifying 3D visual that included such things as flared nostrils, red pupils, a scolding index finger (pointed directly at my hair) and a big, stiff, hairbrush, all belonging to Mother, all set to create havoc. She grabbed me and violently brushed the tangled, hair-sprayed, hairdo until it was just a frizzy mess with no resemblance to the look I had tried so hard to achieve.

Devastated and through tears, I ran up the stairs and placed the teasing comb and can of super hold Aqua Net in a bag. We all left for school. I had ten minutes until the bell rang. I went into the building, tried hard to be invisible, spoke to no one, got to the girl's restroom, and made an attempt to redo the do. Also, I had to repair my makeup since the tears had made my eyes red and smudged my mascara and eyeliner, all of which resulted in a look right out of a Vincent Price horror movie.

Several mornings in a row, I got up early and attempted to fix my hair, but each morning ended the same way, except dialogue was added. In perfect unison, Mother would brush and scream, "You-look-awful-with-your-hair-ratted-it-will-ruin-it-and-fall-out." I watched the hair puddles accumulate at her feet as she brushed away.

Mother made *ratted* sound like a four-letter word. I wondered why Evelyn never received the "hateful hairbrush" treatment.

Mother said I had been lucky enough to be born with good hair, and she didn't want me to ruin it. *Lucky*—is that the word? I thought any luck pertaining to my hair had expired a few years earlier when I convinced my mother to let me get it cut. Oh, what a time *that* had been.

I was almost a teenager. Most of the other girls had outgrown their childhood ponytails. Mine had become longer, thicker, and heavier, nearly outgrowing every size of rubber band. *I could just hear the delivery driver:*

"Got another rush order for a box of Turbo bands to the Faulkner house, STAT—That kid's horse tail had another growth spurt!"

"I thought we quit making those after someone lost an eye."

"Naw, couldn't. Mother threatened to sue. Said her kid's hair was just as valuable as any eye."

Mother would pull that hair straight back and band it so tight that my eyes actually slanted, which made me look like a foreign exchange student. Add a little eyeliner, brows, mascara, a passport, and call me Suzy Wong.

I wanted a short, cute cut—like the other girls had. I began to complain about severe headaches. Mother, ever the pessimist, didn't say it to *me*, but she had a habit of talking to herself. I'm pretty sure I heard her 'whisper' the words "brain tumor." I knew she would. Knowing my mother, she would look it up in one of her medical books and determine "this type tumor" inoperable, rendering the haircut unnecessary. That would leave the mortician more to work with and allow for an overall better viewing experience.

Mother moped around for days. Totally obsessed with my hair, she would take one look at it and almost cry. Mother acted depressed and literally mourned the impending loss. Finally, she told me, in the saddest voice ever, "I have decided that we can get our hair cut."

I was overcome with joy. I couldn't believe it. The next day, I went to school and told everyone I knew that I was getting my first haircut. They couldn't believe I was getting it cut or that it was my first one. After school, I hit the door anxiously asking Mother if she had made the appointment. She told me, "We can't just decide to do it one day and have it done the next."

I asked, "Why not?"

She said, "These things take time; special arrangements have to be made."

I had no clue what she was talking about. I wondered, what could that mean? *Is this going to be some kind of funeral for my hair?* I noticed her serious expression and stopped myself just short of laughing. I might easily have temporarily forgotten her total lack of sense of humor and, on impulse, blurted out the question.

That was too close for comfort. It was the end of any hair discussion for a while.

A few weeks later when I came home from school, Mother announced she had made the appointment. I was closer to being right (about funeral plans) than I could ever have imagined.

The appointment was made at Downtown Foley's with their best stylist. The day after making it, Mother received a card from the salon. It did not offer condolences; however, it did explain their standard operating procedure. Mother read the words to me. They went something like this:

The hair will be cut and sent away to a place where everlasting memories are created.

With tears in her eyes, she glanced up at me accusingly and continued to read:

"It will then be returned to you in its own beautifully scrolled, satin-lined box."

My mother paused, took a deep breath—slowly exhaled—and there was a moment of reverent silence. She closed her eyes for a few seconds. All of a sudden, the whole thing struck me as hilarious. I struggled to keep from laughing. Everything inside of me screamed, "Whatever you do, don't laugh." My shoulders and my body began to twitch and then shake. I held my arms rigid and pressed my hands firmly against my belly, my face became scrunched up while I held my breath. Tears began to form in my eyes. I felt like I was about to explode. I had to have some relief. Suddenly, I flew out of the room, ran upstairs to the bathroom and locked the door. Meanwhile, all I could hear were the words of a smart aleck response screaming in my head, "Now that's a keepsake!"

I ran out of the room so fast my mother thought I had become violently ill. Maybe she thought I had some sort of seizure from the nonexistent tumor she had dreamed up. She was close. I was convulsing with laughter.

When the big day came, we left the house to drive downtown, to Foley's. I had halfway expected to be picked up in a black limo. Apparently, Mother had spoken with the receptionist more than once because she was offered a box of tissue upon arrival and sign-in. She took us to the back immediately. I was thankful. It was best to get this kind of thing started and finished. The procedure would finally be over and done with, and we could begin to move on. The beautician pulled my hair back into its last ponytail, took some scissors, and—*snip!* I felt like the umbilical cord had finally been cut. Once detached, the hairdresser weighed the hefty locks. They weighed in at two pounds. She said, "No wonder you were having headaches."

I was pleased to think I had lost two pounds in that many seconds because of a simple snip of the scissors. It reminded me of a funny greeting card I once read: "Together, Kitty and I weigh one hundred fifty pounds. Have you ever heard of a fifty-pound kitty?"

The best thing was that it would be impossible for Mother to throw the haircut up to me later. She, in good conscience, could not tell me how bad I looked without my red mane. There would be two pounds of evidence curled up in a black, scrolled, satin-lined box to serve as proof, a palpable cause for the (nonexistent) headaches, plus it had been verbally verified, "No wonder you were having headaches." The words still lingered in the air. And the statement had been witnessed by at least three people. I wondered if they had a notary on site.

Fortunately, there was no brain tumor after all. But then, I knew that.

So when my mother "attacked" my head with the hairbrush and reminded me I had been "lucky enough to have been born with good hair," I realized my lucky streak had always placed me right in the middle of torture, turmoil, and torment. The color hadn't helped either. Having red hair always brought unwanted and unfavorable comments, let alone, undue attention. I frequently heard, "Hey, Red!"

I was basically a nameless, faceless, person. "I copied off the redheaded girl. Ask the redheaded girl."

The color of my hair became my identity. At the top of the charts, and my number one favorite was always "I'd rather be dead than red on the head."

My standard comeback was "Yeah, well, I'd rather be red than dead *in* the head."

I was forced to use that so often that I began to utter the response in monotone. For absolutely no good reason, all my life, I had been thrust into a defensive position. Eventually, I gave up on the morning ritual of fixing my hair and just accepted the fact that I had joined the rank of "Scag!" I knew how the girls with first period PE must have felt. Mother made sure that I wouldn't ruin my hair by teasing it. I wasn't allowed to wear it bouffant like the other girls. She preached individualism and didn't care that I never felt stylish with my flat head. She never wanted us to "go along with the crowd."

Even when we became teenagers, we were not allowed to go to drive-in movies or drive-in restaurants. Of course the traditional Galena Park Dairy Mart, Oasis, and Christians, as well as the new Prince's and Ritze, were strictly forbidden. My mother was known to do a drive-through on a regular basis. It was a fact well known, not only to us, but to most of the student body. If she spotted any of us at any of those places, she would drive to the front, get out of her car facing the parked cars, and make a big production of posing while pointing toward the street. She looked like some crazy cop trying to direct traffic at a hamburger joint. Then, she would loudly shout

out our name(s) and order us home at once. The bigger the scene she could make in front of our friends, the more she seemed to enjoy it. She said, "Those are hangouts where teens meet."

Yes! That's why we wanted to go. Mother's ridiculous and endless restrictions were like written invitations to rebellion. Our rebelliousness did not show itself in the form of meanness or evil intentions. It was all in the name of freedom, fun, and fitting in.

Billy's room was next door to mine. After he became a teenager and got his driver's license, lots of nights he placed pillows in his bed and covered them up. That made it look like he was asleep when Mother came upstairs to check on us. And she always did.

He would climb out his window, scale the roof, step down onto the A-frame of our old rusty swing set, and sneak to the side yard driveway. He pushed his truck to the end of the street, jumped in, started it, and was on his way to freedom and fun, hanging out with his friends. I worried so much about him getting caught that I couldn't go to sleep until I heard him open the window. That's when I knew he was safely home.

One Saturday night, Evelyn, my friend Carol, and I decided to test the waters and go to the forbidden drive-in movie theater. Ordinarily, Evelyn wouldn't have gone anywhere with her younger sister and/or her sister's friend, but she had an ulterior motive. We chose the theater carefully, in hopes that Mother wouldn't know its whereabouts. Evelyn and Carol, who were recently banned from seeing their boyfriends, arranged to meet them at the drive-in that night. I, on the other hand, had no one to meet. As dorks would have it, I was satisfied just to go somewhere, eat popcorn and candy, drink Coke, and see a movie. We told our parents we were going to the Capitan (a walk-in theater), and away we went. When we got home, our house was lit up like the Vegas Strip. This was our first clue that our plan might have gone awry.

Mother was standing in the living room with her fluorescent red face, hands on hips, and clearly in attack mode. She demanded, "Where have you been?"

Carol and Evelyn looked at me for the answer. I replied, "At the theater."

"What theater?" she demanded.

"The Capitan," I answered, but my instincts told me this was a setup.

"No, you were not! I drove over there. The car was not in the parking lot," she bellowed.

Why don't I ever listen to my instincts? I took a deep breath, knowing that now I had to follow through with some lame story. Buying time, I calmly responded, "It was there when we left; see, it's in our driveway."

I pointed to the yard and continued to dig myself in deeper. "Maybe someone stole it to joy ride and brought it back before the show was over."

The purported stolen vehicle was a 1954 four-door Olds, "Big Blue," otherwise known as "the Tank," survivor of countless incidents. Yeah, that's the one to steal all right. Unable to contain herself, she drew her hand back and *slap!* My mother slapped me in the face. Holding the injured side of my face, I asked, "Why did you do that?"

She said, "Because you're the one with the friend, and when the two of you get together, y'all are a bad influence on Evelyn."

Insult to injury! I had been the one with no boyfriend—the one who had actually stayed in the car and watched the movie. The three of us were dismissed and were marched upstairs.

Now, by no means am I saying Carol and I were perfect teens; far from it, but at least we were creative. We did enjoy ourselves and sought fun growing up. If we couldn't find it, we made our own. I've often said, "Without Carol or Billy, I would never have had the nerve to do anything."

One time, a teacher told us, "One of you is the *instigator*, and the other is the *troublemaker.*"

I've never been sure who was which, but Carol is the one who dyed her hair green in celebration of St. Patrick's Day. She got expelled from junior high for three days. These days, that would hardly rank as an offense, let alone rate a suspension. I'm pretty sure I saw something like that on the front of a magazine recently.

Once, she and I were passing notes in Ms. Page's health class. I thought Carol had received the note. Unfortunately, at just that moment, Ms. Page appeared from behind Carol, and like a Dallas Cowboy, she had one hand extended to intercept the pass and share it with the class. Both their hands became affixed to the note. There was a three-second stare-off. It all happened so fast, but quick thinking, self-preservation, and desperation forced Carol to rip the note from the teacher's hand, open her mouth, insert note, and swallow. So, for health reasons, if nothing else, (after all, this was health class) we decided to learn sign language from one of those little business-card-looking advertisements given to us in a restaurant by a supposedly deaf person. We became fluent in business card sign language. The new plan had a few bugs to work out. They always do. For instance, if a big kid sat at the desk beside us, it could impair our line of communication and cause a misread.

When Carol went home, the day after our drive-in movie fiasco, her mother said that my mother had rousted her out of the house stating, "Farris (she liked to call people by their last name, except for her friend, Homer May Hale), I don't think those girls went to the Capitan. I have a feeling we were lied to. Ride with me to see if the car is there."

Ordinarily, the car would have been there, as it spent far more time at the Capitan or the Galena Theater than any of us ever did. Both offered great parking facilities and an instant alibi when we hopped into someone else's car to ride around or drive through one of the forbidden drive-in restaurants. But we were going to the drive-in theater. The name alone dictated the use of a car. Mrs. Farris couldn't have known there was a spotlight behind Mother's seat. When she didn't find the car at the Capitan, she proceeded to go to three drive-in theaters, shining the spotlight up and down each row of cars. People were honking and shouting, and probably using their own form of sign language. I'm sure Mrs. Farris scooted herself far down into the seat and wished she could have melted into the upholstery. That's exactly the same feeling we always had when Mother caught us at the drive-in restaurants.

Part of our plan had worked. The slap suddenly felt like a small price to escape the humiliation of having been ... wait for it ... "spotted" by the spotlight.

After that, Mother said we could no longer take Carol to school. When we left each morning, we had to turn the opposite direction of the road to Carol's house, then double back to pick her up.

Slumber parties were a big thing among my friends. Carol usually had the party at her house because her parents were "cool" and actually enjoyed having us over. The party guests included good friends: Pudgy (Mary Shannon), Jeannine Martin, Barbara Kinkaid, Jackie (Yakky) Davis (who rarely said a word), to name a few. Those parties were always great. That was a time when it was safe to "wrap houses" without fear of being shot by the homeowner. In the wee hours of morning, we would sneak out in our pj's to wrap a house. Carol's boyfriend, Murray, was the recipient of many fine "wrappings." We crossed a major street to get to his subdivision, and we were never afraid of anything except getting caught by our parents.

When the phone rang early, at *o'dark* thirty, waking everybody in the house—the morning after a slumber party—it would be my mother. She always came at daybreak to get me. Then I would be questioned about every minute of the previous evening's events. It was impossible to think fast when I was sleep deprived. One time, foolishly hoping to cut the conversation short so I could get some rest, I made the mistake of replying, "Oh, we just sat around, talked, watched TV, and then fell asleep."

"Good," she said. "Then you're not too tired to help me paint a rent house."

After that, my answers became more evasive. I never mentioned sitting, talking, watching or sleeping, unsure of which culprit brought on the painting punishment. That's when I realized, it didn't matter. She couldn't stand slumber parties! Any time I was allowed to attend, I came home tired. I tried to "rest my eyes." She made me sit on the side of the bed and listen to her gripe—a lecture, on and on about everything I had ever done wrong, of which she had total recall, or thought about doing wrong (apparently psychic). Mother obviously thought she could read my mind. Thank goodness she couldn't. That punishment lasted all day. I was not allowed to lie down or sleep until dark. Please, just shoot me! I was not the only victim of this torture. If Evelyn went to a slumber party, she too would endure the torture rack. Sometimes we got the treatment after we returned from a date, as if some of those weren't tortuous enough.

CHAPTER 9

The Banned Band

As a kid, I spent many hours in my room writing poetry and listening to 45s on my record player. Mother loved music and brought records home to me. I think the first 45 I ever *asked* my mother to buy for me was "First Name Initial" by Annette Funicello. I remember wearing a gold chain with an oversized *V.* (Cool, huh?) When I saw the Fabulous Fabian on *American Bandstand* and heard "Tiger," that record became a must-have. Mother took me to see Brenda Lee in person at our new Gulfgate Mall. Like most girls back then, my first love was Elvis. We were tuned in (and turned on) when he gyrated on the *Ed Sullivan Show.*

I loved different music, from country to folk to rock and roll. I mourned the loss of "Gentleman" Jim Reeves, and spent that day alone in my room playing his music over and over again. I cried when we lost the Big Bopper and Buddy Holly. I was totally swept away by "Where Have All the Flowers Gone?" I *became* six-year-old Marie in the song "Memphis, Tennessee."

I loved to sing, and my mother was supportive when I tried out at school functions. She hauled my microphone and speaker equipment, connected to my record player (used for music), to the school auditorium. Once, when it was my turn to perform, part of the electricity went out in the gym. One of my teachers, Mr. Whitaker, tried to coax me to sing anyway, but I refused to go on with the show without my music.

Mr. Whitaker said, "You don't need that music."

I said, "No one needs to hear me sing without it."

That was about the time my friend Carol, (who is a great pianist) and I decided to create our own duo. Both Carol and I had taken piano lessons for several years.

She was a musical guru. She could listen to a record a couple of times, pick out the piano part, and duplicate it, as if she had the sheet music in front of her. She could play anything from, Jerry Lee Lewis to Mozart.

My repertoire of piano tunes lay somewhere between "Chop Sticks" and one hand or the other of "Heart and Soul." With Carol on the bench, we landed a few gigs singing folk music and entertaining at lodges and nursing homes. It was an easy, nonjudgmental crowd. They clapped and sang along with us—not necessarily the same song. We were happy doing that, and it fulfilled our need to perform for a couple of years. Best of all, it gave us lots of weekends to spend time together; singing, laughing, and having fun.

By the time we had reached high school, we wanted to venture out a little more. Carol and I tried out for a school program. We sang "Cotton Fields" in perfect harmony, which seemed to impress our choir director, Mr. Hale. (No relation to Mother's friend Homer Mae.) We were selected to participate. However, before the actual show, we decided to expand our duo and create an all-girl band with piano, guitar, and drums, something we had often talked about. We changed our style to rock, called ourselves the Capris, and the rest is history.

That is true, to a certain extent. The rest *was* history because the day after the school performance, our drill team director called me up to her desk and inquired about our performance attire. She stated, "I heard you girls were wearing skin-tight pants and sheer, see-through blouses." Those words still ring loud and clear in my ears.

I didn't know how to respond. My mother, known far and wide to be the strictest parent in the free world, had gone all over Houston the day before, collecting matching outfits in our various sizes—black stirrup stretch pants, along with aqua, ruffled, *and* lined blouses, with sheer sleeves. To my knowledge, no Weiner's store *ever* carried *exotic* clothing. I was taught to never argue with a teacher, so she probably (to this day) thinks we gave an X-rated performance, unlike the straight-laced can-can dance, choreographed for her drill team officers, who performed it in front of the entire student body. *They* entered the stage whooping and hollering like Ms. Kitty and her band of saloon girls. They were wearing black fishnet stockings with their tightly cinched corsets. An oversized picture of the memorable dance made our school annual that year. I specifically remember because my late, great, dear friend Charles ("Cool Breeze") Dickerson signed his name there. His signature and the words "All my dreams and aspirations lay within this page" are scrolled across Jill's ruffled can-can butt. No, I didn't dare mention that.

Fearing what she might say or do, I decided it best not to divulge this humiliating accusation, with a poor parenting insinuation, to my mother. There's no telling what might have happened. There's one thing I *am* sure of: "Heads would have rolled." The school wasn't prepared for that. Neither was I.

Needless to say, we did not pursue our dreams and aspirations, and the Capris disbanded just after it began. After all, Carol Farris, Linda Parsons, and I were still members (though not in good standing) of the drill team. Mary Shannon (Pudgy) was still in the school band. Strangely enough, we weren't yet ready to jeopardize those coveted positions for the vast unknown world of stardom.

Some of us still get together semiannually to reminisce about the old days and the all-girl rock band and how we could have made it big. It had been our time to shine, stars that we were. But alas and alack, our light was snuffed out. We console ourselves with our motto: "We were before our time."

CHAPTER 10

First Love

After Elvis, my first love was Randy Martin. It was Jeannine's birthday, and her mom took us girls to the Galena Theater. When the movie was over, it was time to pick up Jeannine's brother, Randy, from work. He worked at the drugstore in Galena Park. The four of us walked in and perched ourselves on the bar stools at the soda fountain. That is when I first laid eyes on him. He was cleaning and getting ready to leave. He turned, as if in slow motion, to face us. I saw the finest blond-haired, blue-eyed Troy Donahue–lookin' guy, with a flattop and without the muscles, wearing a red button-down shirt, blue denim jeans, and an ice cream–smeared semi-white apron. I'm sure the shirt was one-hundred percent cotton and machine washable because it looked to be starched and ironed, as did the creased jeans. (Yes, I noticed.) I couldn't see his socks or shoes because he was behind the counter.

We made eye contact. I couldn't help but see that he had (what I call) "laughing eyes." Oftentimes, we see "sad eyes" and "crying eyes." They tell a lot about a person. It is rare indeed when we find a set of genuine laughing eyes. They are the special kind that reflects fun, joy, and happiness. They seem to twinkle, and regardless of the person's age, have actually formed permanent tiny lines at the outside corners from an overabundance of laughter. (See picture of Santa Clause in the book *Twas the Night before Christmas*.) I didn't hear bells, but I swear I heard the song "Today I Met the Boy I'm Going to Marry" when he flashed a mischievous smile my way.

It wasn't long before Randy and I started dating, always double-dating with either his friends or mine. In fact, that's when Carol went on her first date with Charles "Cool Breeze" Dickerson, a date that almost didn't happen.

Charles was running late, so Randy came to get me first. My mother wouldn't have let me go had he been late picking me up. He was with his friend, Donnie Jackson. This was going to be a triple-date, but Carol's parents wouldn't let her go until they met Charles. When we pulled up to Carol's house, I explained the situation to the two of them. Donnie said, "No problem."

He went to the door and introduced himself as Charles Dickerson. They both liked his "clean-cut look" and talked about that later. They were probably impressed by the safe-looking car we pulled up in, Randy's mother's '57 Chevy station wagon.

Carol got to go, but she realized that Charles would never be able to meet her family. We visualized Donnie having to stand in for Charles, should this first date lead to marriage.

Charles was both Randy's friend and mine. He was brilliant, handsome, (he looked a lot like the young Detective Mike Logan, or actor Chris Noth, on TV's *Law and Order*, with the same exact hair) and funny, with a dry sense of humor (more like Logan's side-kick, Lenny). He was adventurous, and although he wasn't "in with the in-crowd," (none of us were) he made it his business to be in the know about the goings-on at Galena Park High School.

One time, Carol was spending a Friday night at my house, and Charles came to get us. He said he wanted to show us something we had never seen before. He took us downtown, and we stopped at a restaurant. We parked across the street and got out of the car thinking we were going to eat at a new place. It didn't take long for us to realize that we were in a gay bar. As we scanned the room, there sat three of our teachers! Charles was right. We had never seen anything like that before. It made going to school on Monday a bit awkward.

When Randy and I weren't together, we were talking on the phone, or he was doing a "drive-by," which meant he was slowly driving past my house. That was my cue to run to my bedroom window and acknowledge him by waving. He did extra drive-bys when Charles came to my house in the evenings to work on our debate topic, "Should the Use of Nuclear Weapons Be Limited to the Control of NATO?" (Charles was my debate partner.)

The drive-bys became more frequent when George Ballew came over to practice our duet acting for the state tournament at Baylor in Waco. We were doing a self-edited scene from Tennessee Williams', *The Glass Menagerie.* Although we didn't win, we made it to the finals, so we performed on stage for all the students. He portrayed the role of Tom, and I was Amanda Wingfield. We certainly didn't realize it back then, but today we would more than likely be called "nerds," not just nerds, more like Green Room Super Nerds! I can visualize our capes. But those are some of my favorite high school memories.

Randy had nothing to worry about except Mother, who listened in on our phone conversations from time to time—most times. When she decided I liked Randy a lot, it was time for her to break up the boyfriend-girlfriend relationship.

One night, he came to pick me up. She rushed to answer the doorbell, mowing everything down in her path, including me. She didn't invite him in. Instead, she told him, "Vickie won't be going anywhere tonight, or any other night, until she learns to squeeze the toothpaste from the right end of the tube."

I guess Randy must have thought insanity might run in the family. He began to distance himself. Besides that, he was scared to death of her. Anyway, we both knew this was not a lifetime commitment, no matter how we had felt about each other. I was heartbroken and stayed in my room the next day. I played "Breaking Up is Hard to Do" over and over, with a little Troy Shondell, "This Time (We're Really Breaking Up)," thrown in for good measure, until I felt I had mourned enough. We went on with our lives, dating other people.

This was not the last time I would see Randy, or that he would remind me of the "toothpaste incident." We passed in and out of each other's lives for years to come, but this had been a time of young love and innocence. It had been a time that would remain in my memory and my heart forever.

CHAPTER 11

The Sixties

The sixties represented a terrific and tumultuous time, to say the least. It was a beautiful fall day, November 22, 1963, just before the Thanksgiving holidays. I was sitting in Van Breman's biology class, talking to Shirley Williamson. The window sills were lined with metal trays. The open louver windows didn't allow much air and did little to prevent the stench of formaldehyde and death from filling the room. Each student was preparing to skin, then label, his or her sacrificial frog—a barbaric and uncivilized, heathenish ritual to which I was highly opposed and said so. I may have been one of the first "conscientious objectors" of the sixties. I remember anonymously posting an eight-inch-by-ten-inch sign on the classroom pegboard declaring, "Frogs have feelings too!" The only response I can recall, due to its cruel and brutal nature, was a cartoon drawing of a line of frogs without legs, exiting a café in wheelchairs. The sign out front of the café announced, "Special of the day, frog legs." Suddenly, we were all stopped dead in our tracks. We received the news over the PA system. President Kennedy had been shot. The previous noise in the room was instantly transformed into a deafening silence.

I looked around the room and saw several students with tears in their eyes. I wondered if they were tears of sadness or fear. I was never a real Kennedy fan, but the idea that we could be a country without a leader was very unsettling. I thought back on past times of bomb drills—how we had been taught to get under our desks and duck and cover. Could the shooter have been sent from some foreign land to terrorize us? Perhaps shooting our president was the first step to another war, or "conflict." It had happened here—on US soil. It was not just the shooting, but the motive behind it, that had me concerned. Later, we found out it had been some lunatic up in Dallas, in our own state of Texas. That night, the world watched it unfold on TV. I felt really sorry for his wife, who witnessed the entire thing. She was sitting in the car next to her husband when the fatal bullet had been fired. Frantically, she tried to stop the bleeding. Inevitably, all she could do was watch as his life slipped away from him and from her.

The country was truly divided in the sixties. Part of the country was protesting for equal rights, part rebelling in the name of peace and love, and part sent to serve their country in Vietnam by Kennedy and then Johnson. I thought we were at "war" in Vietnam. Later we were told it was a "conflict." That conflict took some of my friends and loved ones and brought them back in caskets. If they did come home, many left behind so much of who they had been.

My best friend, Carol, was engaged to Charlie G. He was drafted into the army right out of high school. The night before he left, we had a slumber party at my house, in his honor. Carol, Charlie, Billy, and I stayed up all night, talking. We tried to comfort him and ease his fears. He didn't choose to go; he had to go. He was a kid; we were all just kids. We didn't know much about conflicts or wars.

Unfortunately, we had been introduced to the "sting of death" when early one morning, not long prior to this night with Charlie, our home phone rang. Although her information was sketchy and incomplete, Mother attempted to relay the tragic message to us. She said, "One of the Dickerson boys was killed last night in a car accident."

I was in a state of panic and disbelief. I hoped that my mother had been wrong and that she had misunderstood the last name. It wasn't until later in the day when I talked to Randy that I got the whole story.

Several of our friends, including Charlie G., Randy Martin, and Charles Dickerson, had been out the night before. That night, no different from any other, they were out having a good time. Donnie Jackson was working at the Shamrock gas station, near Jacinto City, on Market Street. The boys skidded into the station to get gas and to make fun of Donnie for having to work on a party night. Ironically,

Donnie said, "You guys better slow down, or you'll end up over there."

Donnie pointed to the Greens Bayou Funeral Home on the opposite corner. They laughed and peeled out onto Market Street, leaving dark black skid marks on the road behind them. They headed toward the old wooden bridge near the end of Wallisville Road. Speed, stupidity, or something caused the driver to lose control of the wheel. The car crashed into one side of the bridge and plunged into the shallow ravine below. Some of the boys were thrown into the floorboard. Part of the bridge, a huge wooden stake (which had served as railing) splintered, broke free, and went flying through the windshield on the driver's side of the car, barely missing the driver. Charles Dickerson was sitting in the back seat, behind the driver. The teens managed to recover their entangled limbs and gain some sort of resemblance to equanimity. Just then, someone turned to speak to Charles. The wooden stake had gone completely through his chest, pinning him to the back seat. He died instantly. The story is almost unbearable. I can't breathe. I can't speak. *I want to scream!* Instead, I retreat to my room, searching for help and seeking answers. I write:

The sudden sting of death,
What sorrow, what agony!
It cuts to the marrow,
It's an irreversible tragedy.
We're taught its part of life,
But *not* how to survive
The sudden sting of death,
It gives no warning,
Leaves no tomorrow,
No plans for the future;
It *reeks* of grief and sorrow.
We're taught its part of life,
Please *help* me to survive.
The sudden sting of death,
So much left to do,

So much left to say,
Plans to get together soon
Suddenly taken away.
We're taught its part of life.
Tell me how do we survive?
The sudden sting of death,
Nothing can explain
This overwhelming pain.
The shadow of death,
The darkness of nothingness,
We're taught its part of life.
Show us how to survive
The sudden sting of death.

This tragedy will remain in the hearts and minds of both Carol and me for the rest of our lives. While she and I continue to age with each passing year, our friend Charles will always be eighteen. Even now, when we speak of him, the mention of his name takes us back to a time of freedom, fun, and laughter, when we were seventeen.

Another student passed away that year. Beth's passing had a profound impact on the entire Galena Park student body. She had participated in a choir contest at another school during the day and became very ill that evening. As darkness began to fall, her temperature began to rise. She was rushed to the hospital, where she passed away that night or early the next morning. The entire school mourned the loss of this sweet-spirited, beautiful, intelligent, young girl. Beth was kind and friendly to everyone who crossed her path. She was admired, respected, and popular. She was voted "Most Athletic" and had been a cheerleader since our days at Woodland Acres Junior High. Not one person was left untouched by her passing. It was *her* death that made us all realize how vulnerable we were, even in our youth. Hundreds attended her funeral. It was later when we "heard" she had contracted meningitis from a contaminated school water fountain while at the choir outing. That year, our school yearbook was dedicated to her memory. The annual contains a large picture of beautiful Beth. Her smile radiates from the page to touch the hearts and souls of her classmates. Anytime I hear the Roy Orbison song "Leah," my thoughts go to Leah Beth Langford, and all the love that was expressed by so many people on her behalf.

With little sleep, having been up all night laughing, talking, crying, and reminiscing, early the next morning, Carol, Billy, and I drove Charlie G. to the bus station. The Shirelles were singing "Soldier Boy" on the radio when he got out of the car.

Charlie was trained as a medic for a short time and then was sent to do his duty. Exactly six weeks after he arrived in 'Nam, he was killed in action, serving his country. Randy was Charlie's best friend. He joined the marines and had already been called to duty. He was allowed to return home so he could serve as a pallbearer for his best friend's funeral. That was the last time I saw Randy for several years.

I'm pretty certain I saw him in a documentary film, *Letters Home from Vietnam*. He was sitting on a log, lighting a cigarette. I know it sounds strange, but it happened to be one of those "letters home" that finalized any hope of a future for the two of us. How rare it is for the person back home to receive the Dear John letter.

His mother and I were very close. She would phone and ask me to come over because Randy was going to call that night. Once, she asked me over to see a picture of his platoon. I remember Jeannine, Randy's sister, telling me that her mother was crazy about me. She added, "I think she cares more about you than she does me."

We laughed about that.

Everybody knows the person their parents would choose is never the one they want. I always figured I would feel the same way, had Mother ever liked even one of my boyfriends. I probably would have thought, "There must be something seriously wrong with him." Obviously, Randy was not the one my mother would have chosen for me. Why else would I have liked him for so long? But then, who was?

I'm sure Charlie had already made several friends. Making friends comes easy when people have so much fear and so much to lose in common. More than likely, he had spent enough time over there for his death to have a permanent effect on a friend who knew him but who survived. It seems to me that PTSD has a lot to do with what one has to do to survive. Then one has to live with the guilt of having survived when friends died. It might be called "survivor guilt" these days, but the bottom line is: it's *still* post-traumatic stress disorder. It was *then*, and it is *now*. Contrary to the often-heard and repeated phrase "Time heals all wounds," rest assured that for some, the mind does not allow time to lessen the pain of loss.

I had a good friend like that. He joined the Marines not long after high school. The rest of his life, he remained close to his buddies, the survivors he served with in 'Nam. His best friend, Gary, was killed in combat. Jimmy never got over the loss. He went through many bouts of depression, not understanding the reason he lived when his best friend and so many others died. In fact, he convinced himself he was unworthy of having lived. I used to tell him, "You are a good person who has not yet fulfilled your purpose on this earth. God makes no mistakes, and He has a plan for you."

Those words seemed to occupy his thoughts for a while, but before long, he would slip right back into a depressed state of mind. When he went there, it was difficult to reason with him, let alone try to rescue him.

People really liked Jimmy. His family adored him. He was kind to everyone he met and was a loyal friend. He had no enemies except himself. He was his own worst enemy. Jimmy did get counseling through the Veteran's Administration. I hoped that would help him. Still, he was either on top of the world or in the bottom of the pits. I thought he was never truly happy unless he was headed to or at one of the marine reunions he attended every year. Death is not the only casualty of war.

My brother, Billy, went. He was one of the blessed ones. He came back in one piece. He didn't like to talk about his time over there. Once I asked him if I could see his awards and commendations explaining what he had done to receive them. Reluctantly, he allowed me to look. Through tears, I read every word and wondered how he maintained his sanity. It had been a time when he did what he had to do and chose not to recall it—a time of innocence lost in the name of survival. I understood.

Meanwhile, my friends and I were safe and secure at home. We were still running the roads, going downtown to a James Brown concert at the coliseum and riding the bus to the Lowe's, Majestic, or Metropolitan theater to see the opening of a new movie.

Our first *James Bond* show was *Goldfinger.* That movie didn't just break former barriers; it destroyed them. I believe it was the first one we girls had ever seen that brought sex, violence, and action to the big screen, all in one package. It was an indication that, as Dylan wrote, "The times they are a-changin'."

The last time I rode the bus downtown on Western Day with the girls was in February 1964. A teenage Hispanic boy saw us walking up the sidewalk. Just as we began to pass him, he reached out and grabbed my crotch. I was at the end of the line, so the others didn't see. I was humiliated and never told anyone about what happened, not even Carol. I had done nothing to encourage such action, yet I felt ashamed. I felt violated. I no longer felt safe.

CHAPTER 12

Stalked

If it had been a familiar word, and we had known what the word *stalking* meant in the sixties, stalkers would have been divided into two groups. We would have had the good ones and the bad ones.

The good stalker would have been a boyfriend who would do a drive-by of your house. He would honk, and you would run to the window to look out. Sometimes a shy boy could use this method to let a girl know he was interested. The next day at school, the girl could brag to her friends, "[So-and-so] drove by my house [such-and-such] many times last night."

This was impressive among girls. That is, unless they thought the driver was someone not worth bragging about.

"High value" bragging rights came as the result of getting your house wrapped with at least twenty rolls of tissue. A count of the leftover cardboard rollers would be necessary to get a total. When the word got out, kids did "drive-bys" to see "high value" wrap jobs. All those streamers were quite an amazing and beautiful sight, especially in the old pastel colors—pink, blue, green, lilac, yellow, and so on.

Then, there was the cleanup. That was not fun, especially if it had rained, and pastel toilet paper lay fading on your parents' white car.

Bad stalking could occur when one broke up with a jealous, controlling boyfriend, and he refused to accept rejection, like one guy I dated the summer before my senior year. I saw him stocking groceries, thought he was cute, and talked to him. Not long after that, we started "going steady." We had fun and really liked each other. He became very serious.

After awhile, I went to work as a checker at Minimax in Jacinto City. There, I met a great guy, Jimmy, who sacked groceries behind me. We talked and laughed a lot. He asked me out, and I wanted to go, but I knew I would have to break up with the other guy first. So I did.

My first date, after he and I broke up, was not with Jimmy. It was with a guy I met at the "Golden Gloves" boxing match, downtown at the Coliseum. We girls went to watch our friend, Kenny Weldon, box. Kenny was a "Golden Gloves Champion."

The guy I met was from Cut and Shoot, Texas. (Yes, it is the real name of a real place.) He wanted to bring a friend who needed a date. I arranged all that, and the boys came to get me first. We headed for Suzanne's house to pick her up. We parked in front. The boys got out and walked up the driveway. As I was exiting, I noticed someone approaching my side of the car. It was my ex-boyfriend. He yelled at me and shoved me back into the car. I stood up, and he hit me, *knocking* me back into the car. He quickly jumped into his vehicle and fled. By this time, the boys were coming back. I had regained my composure. They had been talking as they walked. The two of them had neither seen nor heard what happened. They drove a long way to see us, and I didn't want to spoil the evening for everyone, so I didn't say a word.

We picked up Suzanne and headed downtown. The ex was following us. At that point, I felt it necessary to tell them what had transpired without their knowledge. I begged them to just drive on. We lost him, but the experience was awful. After that night, neither Suzanne nor I ever saw or heard from Cut and Shoot again.

That was the first of many stalking experiences involving the ex-boyfriend. One evening, I was having a Coke at the Oasis drive-in with a friend. He drove by shouting obscenities at us. My friend took me home and got Billy to go help find him, since he had no idea who he was looking for. Meanwhile, the guy speeds through our circular drive, wrecks into my uncle's parked truck, and keeps going.

Another time, he poured sugar into my gas tank. My dad saw the residue before I turned the key to crank the engine. Fortunately, my car survived.

When Jimmy and I did start dating, this same guy went to the grocery store where we worked. He waited for Jimmy to carry out groceries. He grabbed him and held a box cutter to his throat. The police were called. Jimmy pressed charges but later dropped them. We didn't want any more trouble. I guess it worked. He no longer stalked me.

I don't know whether to blame the next stalking or bullying episode on generational curses or "A Bad Moon Rising." It certainly caught me off guard.

Early one summer morning, our telephone rang. I answered. It was a guy who I had known for years. We met at the skating rink when I was in the sixth grade. Back then, I looked up to him and called him my "boyfriend." He spent lots of time at my house. Our families were both local business owners and knew each other.

He had just graduated, and I would be a junior in high school. He called and asked if I would ride to the mall with him. I had nothing better to do so I said yes.

He picked me up, and we left. As soon as we backed out of my driveway, he said, "I forgot my wallet at home."

We went to get it. He opened his car door to get out and said, "Come look at the new room my parents added and the new pool table."

Not giving it a second thought, I got out. I followed him inside and was impressed with the new game room. He disappeared and called me to come help him find his wallet. *Typical guy*, I thought, *can't find anything.*

The minute I stepped into his room, he grabbed me, tried to kiss me, and attempted to push me onto his bed. I pulled away, saying, "Stop!"

"You won't even kiss me?" he asked.

I said, "No!"

He hit me so hard that I fell onto his bed. My ears were ringing so loud that I thought I must have lost my hearing. He left the room. I don't know where he went, but I knew it was time to get out of there.

Earlier, on the way to the game room, I noticed a telephone. I got to my feet, stumbled to the phone, and called my sister to come get me. Neither Evelyn nor I ever mentioned the incident again. We had both been victims of Mother's accusations. We knew that somehow, the entire blame would fall on me, probably for being *stupid*. I was definitely too trusting. This experience did serve to bring my sister and me closer together, and that day I learned she could be trusted.

I guess rejection hit my "sixth-grade *boyfriend*" even harder than he hit me. When school started, in September, I got smirks and Cheshire cat grins from his two younger brothers.

The drill team lined up to go on the football field and perform at halftime. As I marched past the people in the stands, there they were, perched on the railing like two gawking, glaring, grinning gooney birds. I'm not sure what their big brother told them, but I am sure he wouldn't have wanted anyone to know the truth.

Years later, my mother called to tell me that he came by her house for a visit. He asked about me. She said he had been out in Hollywood, "trying to make a star." I do know he was a good actor; he sure fooled me. I seriously doubt he could "make" a star, probably couldn't even get a date with one. Well, Pluto or Ur-anus, maybe … just a little sixth-grade humor.

A year or so after that, I drove to the little store up the road from my house. I went to get milk and bread, so it was a quick run. When I got home, the phone was ringing. I answered. The voice on the other end asked, "Are you the girl who was at the store?" Thinking I must have forgotten something, I replied, "Yes."

The man asked, "Would you come back up here? I want to meet you."

I asked, "How did you get my phone number?"

He said, "I asked the store owner for your name. Then I looked it up in the phone book."

I hung up. I did not feel safe.

I took speech (drama and theater) classes in my first semester of college. When we presented our play, we had to get to the college an hour early. We left late, after cleanup. A friend walked me to my car, and I left on the thirty-mile drive home from San Jacinto Junior College in Pasadena.

I was about ten miles from my house when I first noticed the car behind me. I could see the driver, a man. He was following me. I purposely began to change lanes, weave in and out of traffic, and make sporadic, last-minute turns. He stayed in my lane and made every turn I made. I got home and pulled into my driveway as close to the door as possible. With keys in hand, I jumped out, quickly unlocked the door, and ran inside while calling my brother's name.

The stranger turned into the driveway behind me. He just sat there. Billy got his rifle, opened the front door, and stood on the porch steps with gun in hand. He aimed at the car and was prepared to fire. The car slowly backed out and left.

That experience really did frighten me. There had been lots of talk about how things were "getting worse" and "not like they used to be." I did not feel safe.

I never told my mother or daddy about the frightening chain of events. I wouldn't have been allowed to go anywhere. Besides, my mother always had a way of changing a story around to make things appear as though any negative action was my own fault. Early on, I learned to keep my fears to myself, be cautious, and constantly look over my shoulder.

Reality TV and my now grown-up perspective cause me to look back and realize just how naive and fortunate we were. We didn't know about the existence, let alone the close proximity, of true cruelty and horror until the early 1970s. That's when we heard (for the first time) the names of serial killers Dean Corll and Elmer Wayne Henley Jr.

We learned that Dean Corll lived, and was killed, in Pasadena, Texas. We watched our televisions in horrified disbelief as police unearthed the bodies of twenty-seven boys and young men.

Later, we heard about such nearby happenings as what is now called "the I-45 Murders." The murders took place on a fifty-mile stretch of our Gulf Freeway, from Houston to Galveston, Texas.

That was a beaten path regularly followed by lots of teens on their way to the beach.

It was discovered that bodies were dumped in fields, parks, and waterways along that area. It became known as "the Killing Fields," where over a period of forty-two years, almost that many young girls were murdered or vanished along the route.

It is believed that the I-45 killer first struck in June 1971. It could have been earlier, perhaps in the late '60s. Who would know for sure? The terrain is unforgiving. The killer (or killers) is still on the loose, maybe dead by now. The killings seemed to diminish in the 1990s, when fewer bodies were discovered.

On January 18, 2016, television's *48 HOURS Hard Evidence* aired a detailed program about that "Highway of Hell," south on Interstate 45. They referred to it as a "Ghost story for South Texas," where "truth is more tragic than fiction." The story released names and circumstances familiar to many of us.

Laura Miller disappeared in 1984 after making a phone call at a nearby convenience store. The store was one mile from I-45. In the mid-'80s, police didn't share information, so there was no coordinated effort between departments.

Krystal Baker (the great-niece of Norma Jean Baker, who came to be known as actress Marilyn Monroe) was only thirteen years old when she left her grandmother's house and disappeared on March 5, 1996. Her body was found two weeks later. Krystal's mother, Jeannie Baker, called the Texas City Police. They listed the child as a runaway and would not look for her. It would be fifteen years, in April 2012, before that case could be solved. It was resolved through DNA testing, when the DNA of Kevin Edison Smith was a match. The killer was sentenced to life in prison. Detectives said, "These crimes can be solved."

Laura Smithers was twelve years old when she was abducted from Friendswood, south of Houston. She had gone jogging that morning. Her body was found floating in one of the many area waterways. She disappeared in 1997. They now have a prime suspect in that case. It was the Smithers case that woke up the community and made officials realize these were not isolated incidents. Law enforcement determined it would take combined efforts of police from different locations to resolve and prevent future tragedies.

Only four months later, there was another disappearance. Seventeen-year-old Jessica Cain was abducted. Almost twenty years later, in 2016, police and other officials could be found at dig sites in and around South Houston, searching for her body. They began the dig in February with a plan to search until her remains were recovered. In March 2016, a suspect, William "Bill" Reese, was handcuffed at the site, giving directions as to where the body might have been placed. Finally, in April 2016, bones were discovered at one of the dig sites. They were sent for DNA testing and analysis. It was confirmed that they were, in fact, the remains of beautiful and talented Jessica Cain. The media said friends and family could begin to grieve the loss.

The fear and grief involved in a tragedy like that have got to be the worst-possible nightmare any loved one has to go through. The family would no longer continue to look for her in crowds, on the streets, or in passing cars. I'm sure there is some sense of relief in knowing, but sadly, there is such finality in that knowing. The media said that Reese might also be involved in the death of Laura Smithers.

It is hard to see any good in the face of so much evil, but something good did come about. It was the formation of EquuSearch by a grief-stricken man, Tim Miller, father of Laura Miller, who had disappeared in 1984. EquuSearch continues to be readily available to lead and assist searches for missing persons.

I remember in the late sixties when some moms encouraged their daughters to get married. They said things like "The times are bad," "It's dangerous out there," and "I won't have to worry about you so much when you're married and settled down."

Not *our* mother. Above all else, that was her greatest fear. She hated the thought of it. She never wanted any of us to get married and leave the nest.

CHAPTER 13

Evelyn Gets Married

Evelyn graduated in 1965. She had been dating one person for a long time, and Mother was trying her best to break them up. That had happened before.

Evelyn dated a guy for a year until she was forbidden to see him anymore, for no other reason than Mother decided Evelyn liked him too much.

Life was hard enough without constant parental nagging. At that time, she was a sophomore in high school and could do little about salvaging the relationship. Her boyfriend was a senior and quarterback of our football team, a team that went to the state playoffs that year. He won a scholarship to Blinn College. He would be leaving. His leaving, in addition to the constant battles, was too hard for Evelyn. She finally gave up.

It was Evelyn's junior year when she began to date Jerry. She thought things would be better this time around since our mother and his were friends. That was true—for a little while. Before long, things went back to normal. Mother began to nag Evelyn about "seeing too much of one boy."

Mother made wild and terrible false accusations to them and about them that embarrassed us all. Jerry's mom liked Evelyn a lot. She was kind to her, even though our mother would phone her and say things like "This will end Jerry's college and career ambition because Evelyn might end up in trouble." (Back then, that was code for pregnant!) The two words (*in trouble*) were almost always whispered or mouthed. I prefer to say mimed since that was Mother's particular forte. I thought she said it that way to grab the listener's attention and create an air of mystery. The "mystery air" smelled more like the stench of (silent but deadly) gossip.

She tried her best to destroy the relationship between Evelyn and Jerry. That went on for a long time. Evelyn graduated from high school and got a job. The nagging continued.

One weekend all of us, except Evelyn and Daddy, went to our parents' vacation house in the Texas Hill Country. While we were gone, Evelyn rented an apartment, packed her things, and moved out. I know what a tough decision that was for her. She knew what kind of reaction she would get. And she did. Mother went into a *rage*! Daddy didn't have much to say. Secretly, he told Evelyn that he didn't blame her.

The next morning, Mother made fast work of finding out where Evelyn lived. She ordered me into the car, and away we went. I don't remember where the apartment was. What I do remember is Mother's wild screaming fit about some stolen ice trays (yes, ice trays!) and a pair of Jerry's boots being there. Mother emptied the ice trays and brought them with us. I was happy for Evelyn, but when we left, she was in tears.

Not long after that incident, Evelyn and Jerry got married. They had a pretty church wedding. It would have been perfect, except for one thing—Mother. The wedding pictures speak volumes. (See the lady with the scowl on her face?)

Mother chose for us to show up fashionably late. Really, it had absolutely nothing to do with fashion. I figured she hoped either the ceremony had started so she could interrupt or she could leave and say she didn't want to interrupt since they had started without her. That would be a means of adding more guilt to the equation.

Turned out we were late so she wouldn't have to speak to anyone. She didn't, except once, when Evelyn went to pin the corsage on her. In a loud and hateful tone, Mother asked, "Who's that for?"

Why is it that voices seem to echo in a church?

In her attempt not to draw attention to a possible explosion, Evelyn softly responded, "It's for you, as the mother of the bride."

Mother's loud response was "Oh. Is that what I am?"

Jerry and Evelyn got married June 2, 1966. They have been married more than fifty years.

After they got married, Mother constantly reminded me of how badly Evelyn had hurt her. "Not because she got *married*; I didn't *care* about that. It was because of the way she just moved out without telling me."

Who was she kidding? I was there. I watched the whole thing. I saw how hard she worked to break them up, and I witnessed the wedding. The absurdity of that statement reminded me of a story about a woman who bought a gun for protection from her ex-husband. She placed the gun on a high shelf in her closet and told her daughter to "never, ever touch it."

The drunken ex-husband came to her house. They argued, and he began to choke her. The woman was gasping for air and turning purple. The young girl ran to the closet, got the gun, and shot the man in his behind, saving Mama's life. Afterward, Mama proceeded to whip the girl, explaining, "I'm not whippin' you 'cause you shot your daddy in the ass. I'm whippin' you 'cause you got that gun out of the closet after I told you not to."

My mother's words didn't always make sense either. She had a great way of ignoring her own wrongdoings and placing blame on everybody else. She frequently asked me (in a very whiny, pitiful voice) to promise I would never leave without telling her first. I didn't have anybody special in my life, so that wasn't a hard promise to make. I had no idea how much more difficult life would be for me after Evelyn left.

Mother had been totally dedicated to her *cause*, breaking up Evelyn and Jerry. That had become a lost cause. She no longer had them to concentrate on. That left her with lots of free time on her hands. Billy and I were the only two targets left at home. Billy had a girlfriend. He spent a lot of time with her, and within the year they married. I think Mother always knew she didn't have much control over him. But it didn't keep her from trying, and his wedding—where she was concerned—turned out just like Evelyn's (same woman, same scowl, different dress).

CHAPTER 14

Graduation

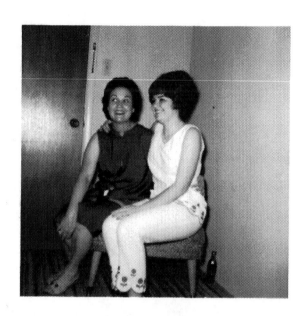

It was the first part of May 1966 when our home phone rang and I answered. The voice on the other end said, "Vickie, this is your mother. I know you graduate this year, and I want to come to your graduation."

I thought about it for a moment and then responded, "Okay." What was I going to say, "No"? It hadn't been a request. It was a statement.

As soon as the "okay" came out of my mouth and passed my lips, I began to create all kinds of mental scenarios and what-ifs. What if it rained? There were nowhere near enough seats in the auditorium to accommodate entire families. I was sure we would only be given two tickets, one for each of our parents. Back then, most kids didn't have multiple moms. And if I could get more tickets, wouldn't that place all of them on the same row next to one another? I felt certain it would all be done alphabetically—by the kid's last name—like everything else having to do with school. Great! That would place Carol's parents, the Farris's, in the two seats before Mother and Daddy. That was good. They would make excellent witnesses to whatever might happen. Oh no! Daddy would allow Mother to be seated before him. Dale and Gloria would enter from the other side of the aisle (because that's just my luck). Dale would be behind Gloria. That would place Mother and Gloria in seats next to one another. Could it get any worse?

On a more optimistic note, it *had* been years, so maybe they wouldn't recognize one another. The auditorium would probably be dimly lit since everyone would be focused on the graduates. More than likely, lights would be directed that way. Could it get any worse? *Yes!* I conjured up the audio and visual of how it might all go down.

Mother: "Hello. I guess you have a child graduating tonight?"

Gloria: "Yes, I do. We're so proud."

Mother: "So are we ... and thankful. This was one we weren't sure about." (???)

Gloria: "Oh, we were always sure. She'll probably graduate with honors." (???)

Mother: "Lucky you. What's her name?

Oh, horrors! I shudder at the thought!

Just then, I could hear Gloria repeating, "Hello ... hello ... Vickie, are you there?"

"Dale, did this phone disconnect?"

I responded, "I'm here, I'm here."

I gave her the date. She asked me if I knew anyplace to stay when she and Dale came. I told her I would look around, make reservations for them, and call her back. I got her phone number.

I told Carol. She was excited to finally get to meet the lady in the picture. The one she had seen all those years ago. I had been apprehensive at first, but as time drew closer, I became more excited about getting to see her again. Carol and I made the reservation, and I called Gloria to let her know the plans.

Traditionally, after graduation, kids would go to all-night parties. Gloria and Dale took us to Kemah to eat. We went back to their room where we visited for several hours, getting to know one another. We made plans to see them the next day. They stayed for a few days and then headed back home to Michigan. It had been a good visit.

It was fifty years later when I found out that Aunt Doris had also attended my graduation.

I had applied to and had been accepted to a few Texas colleges, but I wasn't allowed to go. Carol begged me to go with her to Lamar Tech in Beaumont. It was close enough for her parents to get to her if she needed them, yet far enough to be on her own. I wanted to go and was disheartened but not surprised when my mother told me no. She said, "If you want to get an education, you can stay right here and go to San Jacinto Junior College. I'm not paying for you to go away."

I didn't have many friends left at home. All my guy friends had either been drafted or had joined some branch of the service. My girlfriends were either getting married or going away to school. I told Mother that I was thinking about becoming an airline stewardess. She told me I was too short. More for shock value than anything else,

I said I was thinking about joining the military. I hoped that would scare her into suggesting I go on to Lamar Tech with Carol—no ... that she would *beg* me to go. Completely oblivious to my comment, she said, "You always wanted to be a teacher."

She was right. But now, I had decided that I wanted to be on my own for a while.

One night, Gloria and I talked on the phone about my desires for the future and my rejected plans for college. I told her how nice it would be to "go away." She asked me to come there and go to Michigan State. She said, "Dale and I will pay for your college, and we will buy you a new Mustang. You will have your own bedroom. I bought your bedroom furniture several years ago, in case you ever wanted to come live with us."

I wondered if she had bought the furniture before or after she came to Houston to visit me eight years earlier. If it was before, had she planned on taking me home with her? Also, I wondered how she knew the Mustang was my dream car. Then I remembered telling her. Right after the car was released, Billy and I headed to the nearest Ford dealership to peer through the window and drool over the new birth. We picked up a full-color brochure. The centerfold was gorgeous—a sleek and shiny Mustang. She had an ivy green exterior with ivy gold interior. Billy framed and hung that awe-inspiring, spectacular two-page centerfold on his wall like it was Ms. July. On the way back home, we devised a plan as to how we might acquire the sensational beauty. We knew it was fail proof because it worked in a movie we once saw.

We went home, dug through our closets, and found our old tape recorder. That evening, the two of us recorded, over and over again in a continuous loop, every desired available option. When Mother finally fell asleep, we slid the recorder with the taped messages under her bed and set it to Play. It played all night. The repetitious message would plant the seed firmly in her subconscious mind. Surely, by early the next morning, we would be headed to the dealership to pick it up. But we weren't. Mother never mentioned anything about a car.

We couldn't understand why our fail proof plan hadn't worked. After much deliberation and debate about what might have gone wrong, we arrived at a conclusion. It had to have been Mother's loud snoring. We determined that the snoring had drowned out our subliminal messages, thereby causing a complete and total system failure.

About a week after that phone conversation with Gloria, I received an anonymous package in the mail. I guessed it was a graduation gift from some unknown distant relative who had received one of my many invitations. As soon as I opened it, I knew who it was from. Gloria sent me the record "Did You Ever Have to Make Up Your Mind?" That was funny, and the offer was wonderful, but I couldn't go. I wouldn't hurt my mother like that.

CHAPTER 15

The Last Straw

The summer after I graduated, Evelyn decided to sell her car, an older four-door Ford Fairlane. Mother bought it for me to go back and forth to college at San Jacinto. It was my first car, and I liked it a lot. It wasn't the Mustang, but it was nice and offered a little freedom. I wouldn't have to ask friends for rides. Best of all, my mother wouldn't be dropping me off or picking me up from college.

I met Bud that summer. He came to Houston from Kentucky. His mother, Mary, rented a house from my mother. He'd served four years in the navy and had come to Houston to work with his brother-in-law. I liked that he was older, twenty-six. I was eighteen. He was handsome, funny, and easy-going. Every Friday evening, Bud took me to dinner at the Satellite restaurant in Pasadena. They had good food and great music. There was a jukebox, and each booth had its own selection box on the table. We would flip through the songs and play our favorites. We both loved Merle Haggard and his latest song, "The Fugitive." We always chose it with our three 45s for a quarter. It wasn't long before we had our own special song: "Walk through This World with Me" by George Jones.

I enjoyed going out with Bud. When the fall semester started, I went on to San Jacinto Junior College. Sometimes he would drive the thirty-mile trip there, just to take me to lunch. The attention made me feel pretty special.

The days were long at college because of theater practices. One night, Corinne, a girl in my class, asked me to drive her home because she couldn't get a ride. I said, "Sure."

I had no idea how far away she lived, and I got lost on my way home. There were no cell phones back then. No one wanted to stop at a pay phone because they were usually dirty and disgusting. I thought about stopping to call, but if I did, I would have to hold the receiver so far away from my mouth that my mother wouldn't be able to hear me. That late, the only thing a phone call might accomplish would be to worry her. She might get in her car and drive all the way to the college, or worse, she might call the police. Besides, getting out in a phone booth at almost midnight was pretty scary. That scene had been used in too many horror movies. I decided it was best to drive on.

When I did finally get home, my mother was livid. She demanded to know where I had been. I tried to explain to her, but she kept yelling until Daddy got mad. They both thought I was lying, and Daddy screamed at me. My daddy had never screamed at me before. I ran up the stairs to my room. He stood at the bottom of the stairs and demanded my car keys. I tossed them down. Daddy must have thought I was acting belligerent. I wasn't. I just didn't want to get within arm's reach of Mother. Then Daddy called me a "dirty bird." Yes! His exact words were "You … you … dirty bird." Then Mother flew in after me. I was used to Mother's yelling and preaching, but my daddy's two words cut deep. Looking back, I can see that Daddy probably displayed a great deal of restraint with the words *dirty bird*. In fact, they strike me as pretty funny now, having seen Kathy Bates in the movie *Misery*. Anyway, Mother was so mad, and once again, I tried to explain. She would not give me a chance. Loudly, I asked, "Why are you screaming? I can hear you!"

That really did it. Even louder, she screamed, "I'm not screaming! I don't scream!"

My response was, "Oh, yes, I remember now; you *never* scream. I'm supposed to say that you are speaking in a 'loud voice.' Sorry, I guess that must have slipped my mind."

Whoa. She blew a cork! She turned red as a beet. I thought she might have an aneurysm right then and there. I couldn't take this anymore. I picked up my telephone and dialed Bud's number. In a flash, my mother was standing in front of me with steam coming out of her ears. She was midsentence when he answered my call. I asked him, "Do you still want to marry me?"

He said, "Yes."

I said, "Okay."

Oh, the sweet sound of silence, if only for a few seconds. My mother was just winding up for another one of her all-night squawking sessions. Cuckoo! Cuckoo!

I didn't get my keys back, so I rode to college with Bud's brother, Philip, the remainder of the semester. The next summer, I applied for, tested, and got a job at Houston Lighting and Power. My sister was working downtown, so I rode with her.

Bud bought an engagement ring for me. It was precious, a bow with a diamond in the center. Mother asked to see it. I took it off and handed it to her. She pulled it up within a couple of inches from her eyes as though searching for the diamond, and then she threw it across the room. Next, she threw her rent receipt book at me (*Incoming!*), which hit me in the head. It wasn't your ordinary, flimsy, little single receipt to a page, three-by-five-inch receipt book. Oh no. This was a big, black, hardcover, four-to-a-page, ten-by-thirteen inches, with duplicates, receipt book. It compared (in size) to Mother's medical book, which contained definitions and extensive information about every illness and disease known to mankind, most of which she thought she had. That was the book she used to self-diagnose. The thing might have weighed nearly fifty pounds. I could have gotten a concussion. (I looked it up in the medical book.)

One evening, Mother sat in her Windsor rocker, with her back turned to everyone. She just sat there, facing the living room window. (Why am I reminded of the Hitchcock movie *Psycho*?) She watched out the window until she saw Bud's car pass, when he returned home from work. She waited about an hour and then demanded that I walk to his house with her. She knocked on the side door calling, "Mary," as she boldly pushed it open. Mary, Bud's mother, had been asleep and woke up wondering what was going on. I was wondering the same thing. Bud was sitting at the kitchen table with a sandwich and a glass of milk. Mother walked over, picked up the glass, and sniffed it. Bud asked her, "Alma, would you like a glass of milk?"

She became furious.

Mary came into the kitchen and said, "Why don't we all go into the living room and sit down."

Mother said, "I don't want to sit down!"

The rest of us moved into the living room. Mother followed. She stopped and stood beside the front door. Mary asked, "What's wrong with you, Alma?"

Mother replied, "These two are making me crazy."

Mary said, "Well, I think they are. You're wearing two different shoes."

She was. (Why couldn't I think that fast straight out of slumber?) Mother has a tendency to go berserk when she gets really mad. She doesn't care what she says or who she hurts. She told Bud, "You're not getting a virgin: she won't bleed."

What? Where did that come from? At that moment, I realized why we were there. It was to humiliate me in front of Bud and his mother. She did a great job—I was totally humiliated—but the worst was yet to come. I got up out of the chair and walked to the door to leave. Bud watched me as I was leaving, and Mother said, "Yeah, I bet you want to f—— that."

I left. I didn't know what else she might have said, but she got home a few minutes later and came into my room yelling. She kept me up all night. Among many things, she said, "You'll never have a thing. Don't look to me for help. I'm not giving you anything. I don't care if you starve to death."

Her most hurtful words were "You came from nothing. Without me, you would have had nothing. You *owe* me."

It took a minute for me to absorb those words. I heard what she said, but somehow my ears, brain, and heart had become disconnected. Suddenly, every crippling feeling that I ever had surrounded me like a shroud. My mind was beginning to malfunction. My face and lips felt as if they were becoming numb. Something wasn't right. I felt that I was losing control of my mind and my body. It was as if everything I thought to be real had been nothing more than lies. I forced myself to try and cope. I searched my frazzled mind. If I could just find truth in something, then I would be able to cope.

Without a single tear, I calmly responded, "You always said how important your children are to you and how much happiness they brought you. If all that is true, what could we owe you?"

Mother sold my car that week. She made Mary and her family move.

The next day, Billy and I were sitting in the dining room, eating a bowl of macaroni and cheese. Mother came in, gave me a dirty look, picked up my bowl, and dumped the food on top of my head.

Billy jumped out of his chair and pushed her away.

A couple of days later, the phone rang. I answered. It was my birth father. I hadn't remembered talking to him or seeing him since I was about three years old. That's when he dumped me with a new mother and took off.

I did remember that once—when I was very young—he came by and picked me up. He took me for a ride in his brand new convertible. He drove through the Washburn Tunnel with the top down. A kid doesn't forget a thing like that.

While on the phone, he asked me if I saw him pass by my house.

I said, "I wouldn't know who you are."

"I was the one driving the eighteen-wheeler. I saw you outside, and I slowed down. I threw a book of matches out the window."

I hadn't seen any of that. I was a teenager. I had tunnel vision. Had the matches ignited and blown the truck up, *that* I probably would have noticed.

He asked me if I could drive to Carlton's store on Federal Road.

How am I going to do that without a car?

He said, "I have a graduation present for you."

Maybe it is possible. I told him I'd try.

I humbled myself and asked to borrow Mother's car to go get milk.

"Straight there and straight back" resonated throughout the house.

Nervously, I pulled into the parking lot. I did not feel safe. He got out of his truck, came over, and got into the car. The conversation went like this:

Him: "Vickie, I have to tell you that I never signed any adoption papers."

No response from me.

Him: "Are you afraid of me?"

Me: "No."

Him: "Then why are you shaking?"

No response from me. I was terrified!

Him: "I want to give you this for graduation."

He handed me a crisp, new one-hundred-dollar bill.

Me: "Thank you."

I didn't say anything else, but I was thinking, *With this money and the sale of my bicycle, I would have enough for Bud's wedding band.*

He said, "Goodbye."

He got out of my car and left.

For so long, I regretted having accepted the money, feeling I had "sold out" cheap to a man who had abandoned me. Could this pittance somehow serve to ease his guilt? Did he have any feelings of guilt? I pledged to myself, *If I ever see him again, I will give it back.*

CHAPTER 16

Jim Goes Home

When Billy got married the same year as the rest of us, it was like déjà vu of Evelyn's wedding. Mother couldn't stand to lose her little boy to another woman. I couldn't stand to lose my brother to war. I knew that once he dropped out of college, he would be drafted. He was. First, boot camp, and then straight to Vietnam, where he served on the front lines in the midst of constant battle. He watched men die and worked hard to stay alive. I prayed for him all the time.

Billy wasn't the only one I was praying for. My brother Jim was over there too.

During the Christmas holidays, 1966, Bud and I had gone to eat at Walt Williams's on Market Street with some friends. I had only talked to Gloria a couple of times since she came to my graduation in May. I excused myself from the table and went to the pay phone to make my collect merry Christmas call. I was pleasantly surprised when Jim answered the phone. He identified himself and said he was home on leave. I had not heard his voice in eight years. I would never have recognized it—so deep and grown-up.

Jim had only been twelve years old when he, Harold, Gloria, and Dale visited me in Houston those years ago. It was hard to believe the twins, my brothers, Jim and Harold, would soon be twenty-one—on January 3, 1967. I would remember and cherish that phone conversation for the rest of my life.

Jim told me, "Mom has your graduation picture on the mantle of the fireplace. Today, I picked it up and said, the minute I get out, I am coming to Houston to see you."

He knew he was on his way to Vietnam, but at that moment, he was filled with faith, hope, and love. I told him I couldn't wait to see him, and I would pray for him every day. I wrote to him, and he wrote back. I still have his letter.

Several years ago, I misplaced the letter. I searched everywhere for it. A couple of months later, I was moving and had just finished packing. The only two things left in the house were the lawn chair I was sitting on and one, unused, empty box. I picked it up to disassemble it. There on the floor, beneath where the box had stood, was the letter I had not seen in almost twenty years. I couldn't help but smile as I picked it up, removed it from the envelope dated 1967, and reread each word. Finding that letter was no less than a miracle. It appeared at just the right time and had my undivided attention. That was as close to an actual visit as we would ever get. I felt that Jim fulfilled the promise he once made to me in a telephone call.

Death in Vietnam Breaks Promise

'Shimmy' Won't Return to See Beth

Beth Ann Mitchell, 4, knows Lance Cpl. Jimmy O. Barnes, 21, son of Mr. and Mrs. William Campbell, 1015 N. Logan St., will never come to see her as he promised he would.

Barnes was killed Saturday in Vietnam.

Beth Ann, daughter of Mike Mitchell, Barnes' best friend, was special to Cpl. Barnes. She always called him "Shimmy." Mr. and Mrs. Mitchell reside at 4110 Hillborn St.

Beth recently received a poem from Cpl. Barnes. He called it "Beth's Shimmy." Barnes wrote:

"There is a girl that's dear to me,
She's as pretty as can be.
She's only about four feet one, not one.
No other girl can compare,
Yes, Beth, it's you and there's no doubt.
Yes, it's you I say these things about.
Just keep on calling me your 'Shimmy,'

For that's the only way it should be.

And one day very soon you see,
There will be a knock at your door and.
Guess what? It's me, Your "Shimmy."

Yes, it will be me at your door,
Never to go to war no more.
So say a li'l prayer for me,
And I will see you very soon.

Love, your "Shimmy"

Cpl. Barnes, a lineman in a communications section, was a member of H and S Company, 1st Battalion, 9th Regiment, Third Marine Division. He arrived in South Vietnam seven months ago and was stationed at Con Thien.

A 1965 graduate of J. W. Sexton High School, Cpl. Barnes attended Lansing Community College. A member of the South Baptist Church, S. Washington Avenue, he was employed by the Hausman Corp., before entering the service.

The marine enlisted in April 1966 and received his basic training at San Diego, Calif. After completing his basic training, he was transferred to Okinawa before being reassigned to South Vietnam.

Related Story Page C-7

CPL. JIMMY BARNES

Jimmy was engaged To Arlene Deuel. Her older sister Carol was married To Mike Mitchell. They had 2 children. Beth oldest and Sheri youngest.

He wrote This poem To Beth and it was published in the Lansing State Journal.

Lance Corporal Jimmy O'Neal Barnes, United States Marine Corps, was killed in combat, July 8, 1967, in Con Thien, Vietnam.

I don't remember who notified me of Jim's death. It must have been Harold. I had only been married for four months and six days. The one thing I *did* know was I had to go to Michigan. I didn't know how I was going to get there or how to break the news to Mother, but I had to go. I called her.

I couldn't afford to fly, so I checked bus fares. Since age three, I had never been out of the state of Texas and had no clue how far it was to Lansing, Michigan. Before now, I never needed to know. The near invisible tiny pin mark where I hung my US map back at home had been both safe and satisfactory for me.

On the morning I was scheduled to leave, Mother called and insisted she ride with Bud to take me to the station. All the way downtown, she made statements like "You'll never come back home" and "You will get up there and stay."

I asked her why she thought I would leave my family. I said, "Mother, I just got married. Why do you think I wouldn't come back?" She didn't give me an answer.

I think I must have ridden a dozen or more buses to get to Michigan. It seemed like I changed buses at every station between here and there. I don't remember feeling unsafe. I always chose the seat behind the driver so I could ask questions before the next stop. I worried more about getting on the wrong bus than anything else.

When I arrived, days later, Gloria and Dale picked me up from the station. I was totally exhausted but glad to finally get there. Before that day, the address on North Logan had only been numbers written on a piece of paper—one I had carefully hidden and carried inside my purse for a very long time. Now it was real. It was the address of a real house, on a real street where my real family had lived for years.

Harold and his wife, Virginia, were waiting there for me. Gloria, Dale, and I entered through the side door, stepped into the kitchen, and walked into the living-dining area. My eyes scanned the room to the fireplace where my graduation picture remained on the mantle.

Gloria went upstairs to her room.

Dale took my bag up.

I walked over and picked up the picture. I guessed I was probably standing in about the same place Jim had stood, only a few months before. My fingers lightly touched the eight-by-ten-inch frame as I traced its outline. Knowing Jim had been there, holding the picture, gave life and reality to an otherwise surreal situation. It made me feel close to him, standing where he had stood; touching an object he had held. I remembered the words he said in our last conversation—his *first* and *final* phone conversation with me: "Mom has your graduation picture on the mantle of the fireplace. Today, I picked it up and said, the minute I get out, I am coming to Houston to see you."

Picture of house on North Logan in Lansing, MI. This was home of Gloria and Dale and where Vickie visited when Jim was killed in 1967. Gloria and Dale lived there from the 1960's until they moved back to Memphis, Tennessee in the early 1980's.

That night, Harold, Virginia, and I sat around the small kitchen table, drank coffee, and talked. Harold told me stories about Jim and their lives together. He told me one story about how he got Jim and himself into big trouble by a simple little white lie.

The two boys rode the bus to and from their country school. When they returned home after a long day, Harold asked the bus driver to wait. He was going to run inside and ask Aunt Eva's permission for the two of them to ride to their friend's house and stay the night. The only person at home was a relative who had no authority to give approval. In fact, he told Harold, "You better not go."

Somehow, Harold must have misinterpreted his words. He ran back to the bus, jumped on board, and informed Jim, "Yes, we can go."

At six o'clock, the boys, their friend, and his family had just sat down to supper.

Aunt Eva came knocking on the door. She had come to retrieve them and was plenty mad. She ordered both the boys into the car. On the way home, she threatened to take Jim and Harold directly to the police station. She said they had broken the law. They had both been bad and were now considered runaways. Aunt Eva slowly approached the driveway but kept going.

The twins visualized their pictures on Wanted posters. They were terrified to think they might have to face a bounty hunter or serve jail time. Neither of the boys said one word. Since they were twins, each one usually knew what the other was thinking without saying a word. The car began to slow down, and Aunt Eva was paying more attention to the lesson she was trying to teach than to what they were doing. As though their next action had been precisely planned, the boys, in total synchronization, reached for their door handles, pulled up on them, and jumped out of the car. They ran through the tall cornfields and sneaked into the house through the back door. Once there, they quickly put on their pajamas and hopped into bed.

Could they possibly have thought she believed they were asleep or cared if they were? She went into their room, threw the covers back, and proceeded to whip the bottoms of those runaway *Children of the Corn* with a belt. Later, she apologized for having "worn them out." She added, "But it was better comin' from me than from Big Daddy."

Harold talked a lot about spending time with his grandfather, Big Daddy, at different sawmills. He said they worked hard, but it was lots of fun. Sometimes, they got to travel with him to other states. He remembered going to Arkansas. Harold told me, "We would help out by keeping the sawdust piles down with a shovel. By the end of the day, we looked like two big piles of sawdust with eyes."

Harold talked about Gloria, with her great sense of humor. He said they could always make her laugh, even if she was mad at them. He told me that every year, on their birthday, January 3, Gloria always baked a big coconut cake, their favorite. I thought about asking if she had ever remembered *my* birthday. Had she ever baked a german chocolate cake in my honor? But how could she have known about my favorite cake, or for that matter, my favorite anything?

The stories were bittersweet. A part of me was envious, because I had not been there. I didn't know why I ended up in Houston when Gloria had raised the boys. I knew just enough to feel hurt and rejected. I wasn't very tolerant of anyone who could give his or her child away, and the three of us discussed my innermost feelings on the subject.

Harold said, "We grew up knowing we had a sister in Texas; Mom never let us forget it. We loved you and wanted you with us, but we were just kids and could do nothing about it."

I was deep in thought about those words. I saw the hurt in his expression and heard it in his voice. I thought they represented his desperation to reassure me of their love, and his exasperation, knowing "actions speak louder than words," when no adult came forward to do anything about it. Just then, I noticed Virginia staring at me. I was certainly in no mood for her (next) shallow, off-the-wall comment, "You don't look like your graduation picture."

Where did *that* come from? Had she been watching me earlier when I took the picture off the mantle? Did she think I was admiring it? Did she think I was an imposter? And, for that matter, who cared what made her come to that conclusion? I *wanted* to ask her how in the world that could be. Could it be that I had ridden buses for days, got little to no sleep, lost a brother I would never know, worried that Gloria might not survive the tragedy, and left my mother on a bus station curb thinking I would never return? Not to mention, I needed a bath, shampoo, and makeup in the worst possible way. I probably didn't *smell* like I did on the day my picture was taken either. Why didn't she just throw that in too? Yes, Virginia, let's discuss my unsightly appearance. Instead, I told them "good night" and went upstairs.

I opened the door to my assigned room and discovered a beautiful new antique-white and gold bedroom suite with a canopy bed.

Upon closer inspection, a few minor imperfections indicated that the furnishings were probably not brand new. That's when I realized, *this had to be the furniture bought for me nine years earlier.* It still looked and smelled brand new, and the care and gentle use it had received, reminded me of the *old-new* dolls and toys from my childhood. They are the ones that remain nearly perfect and continue to sit on a high shelf in my home.

Sadly, all of them—the child, the toys, this room, and those who entered it and left—missed out on so much childhood joy and happiness, two of God's greatest gifts. This room did look and smell new—near-perfect—but perfection costs dearly. The room had never been doused in the sweet fragrance of a young girl's perfume, never heard secrets shared between best friends, and never had the freedom of simple silliness at a girls' slumber party. It had never worn the frilly ruffles of pink curtains and never felt the softness of a lace bedspread. At one time, this room had been filled with the hopes and dreams of a mother who waited for a daughter who would never arrive.

Gloria was glad to see me, but she was overcome with grief. She went upstairs to her bedroom and didn't leave again the entire time I was there. I went up to see her. She didn't talk much, so I just lay down beside her and hoped my presence offered some sort of comfort.

After a couple of days, we were notified that Jim's body had been delayed. It was unknown as to how long it would take to arrive. I waited for a few days and realized it might be a week or more before he was returned to his family. I don't remember how long it took, but I had to get back home to my family and job. I called my mother.

She eagerly offered to pay my airfare so I could get home faster. I was both thankful and relieved that I didn't have to take the long bus ride home. I didn't want that much free time to think.

I was only nineteen years old when Jim died. At the time, I felt so much guilt about one of my prayers: "If only one of my brothers can come home, please bring Billy back." I carried that guilt for many years until I finally understood that God doesn't make deals. He creates miracles.

CHAPTER 17

Baby Boy

*Only be careful, and watch yourselves closely so that
you do not forget the things your eyes have seen or let
them slip from your heart as long as you live. Teach them
to your children and to their children after them.*
— Dt 4:9

On February 18, 1969, I learned the meaning of unconditional love when I gave birth to my son, Jim. Despite the warning my mother gave as they wheeled me into the delivery room—"You better get your heart right with God; lots of women die during childbirth"— things went well. I had a healthy redheaded baby boy. I felt more complete than I ever felt in my life. I had something very special to call my own. That day, that year, just happened to fall on Western Day, which is a very big deal in Houston, Texas. I drifted off to sleep and dreamed of the excitement and cheers at the parade in celebration, not of rodeo, but of this amazing new arrival.

The next morning, Bud came to get us. It was a very cold, rainy day when the nurse placed baby Jim in my arms and pushed the wheelchair to the parking lot. The nurse held the baby while I got into the car. She passed the precious blanketed bundle to me and said these profound words: "Enjoy him. They don't stay little for long."

Looking back over the years, at the times we have shared and continue to share, I know he has been the real joy of my life. It is truly a privilege to call him my son and my friend.

Throughout the years, I have been given advice and opinions on child-rearing. Early on, it was much appreciated. I had never been around a baby, never changed a diaper, and knew nothing about all the work, patience, knowledge, and common sense involved. I couldn't call my mother to ask her. She never had a baby. She didn't much like them. Once, we were in a family restaurant (a cafeteria), when a baby began to cry. Mother actually asked, "Who let that *baby* in here?"

Some of us are lucky our babies survived. They don't come with instructions.

Case in point: My doctor told me to give Jim his vitamins every day. I asked him, "How do you give vitamins to a baby?" He answered with an "I hope you're kidding" look on his face, "In his bottles." When we got the prescription filled, I realized the vitamins were liquid (duh). The baby began to have recurring diarrhea. Everyone couldn't afford to use disposable diapers back then, and we couldn't wash the cotton ones fast enough to keep up. Worried that something must be wrong, I called the doctor's office and explained the situation to the nurse. I told her that I was doing everything they told me to do, including putting vitamins in his bottles. She said, "You're only supposed to put them in *one* bottle a day."

I was making my baby sick. Why don't people say what they mean? Talk about postpartum depression. I began to wonder what else I might be doing wrong.

We didn't use car seats. Some cars didn't come equipped with seatbelts, especially the old used ones that most of us had to drive. How did our children ever survive? Come to think of it, our parents didn't have any of those safety devices either, and aren't we the overflowing baby boomer generation, alive and well, getting ready to drain Social Security funds?

I have heard the question asked, "Why would anyone choose to bring a child into this terrible world?" Call me selfish, but I can't imagine a person living life to its fullest potential if they never experience the fulfillment that comes with having a son or daughter, not to mention grandchildren. If that person left this earth today or tomorrow, neither he nor she would have had the remarkable opportunity to give or receive that kind of unconditional love. Why would anyone not want to experience everything good and wonderful that life on this earth has to offer, if it is within their power to do so?

I don't know exactly how to explain the unexplainable. It's a real struggle, finding the right words to describe the bond between Jim and me. Maybe it's because I only have one child. No, that answer doesn't feel right. Okay, maybe it sounds a little crazy, but I'm sure I am not the only woman who has "the Gift." For all practical purposes, it is a *gift*, a phenomenon of sorts. It is the ability to *know* something, without knowing *how* you know it. I said it sounded a little crazy. I guess the simple way to put it is, "mother's intuition."

More than likely, there are those who don't believe in such things. In that case, maybe they could help me explain this: Jim was about twelve years old. He loved to race his bike at the track in Conroe. Bud and I took him almost every weekend. At that time, we owned a rent house in Greens Bayou. There had been a hurricane a few weeks earlier, and a huge oak tree fell in the yard. We had the tree cut and removed, but it damaged the back of the house. I asked a friend if Jim could ride to the races with them while we stayed to make the necessary repairs.

We were scraping the back of the house, getting it ready to repaint, when out of nowhere I was stricken with a deep feeling of dread. I put the scraper down and said, "Bud, something has happened to Jim. He has been hurt."

At almost the same moment, my mother wheeled into the driveway. I met her at the car. She said, "Jim has been hurt. Wanda called and told me to have you get hold of a dentist because his front teeth were knocked out, and they can't get the bleeding to stop."

That was my first "insight" encounter. It was like a *Twilight Zone* experience.

The next time it happened was years later. I should mention that in between times, Jim missed one or two events due to my feeling of dread. I remember when his best friend, Jimmy, got his new car and wanted to pick him up to go riding. It wasn't a fast sports car or anything like that. In fact, it was a four-cylinder, four-door sedan. I said, "Jim, I don't feel good about you going."

I guess the strangest thing was that he didn't argue with me. Jimmy came by to show off the car, but Jim didn't go with him.

I think his friend's ride was uneventful, and he got home safe and sound.

Anyway, several years later, Jim and Stefanie were married and expecting. They had just built a new home in Crosby. He had his dream garage, and he was piddling around in it. Bud and I were sitting on our patio, thirty miles away, in Woodforest, in North Shore. I had taken the phone outside with me, and I called Jim to check on Stefanie. We were about to hang up when Jim said, "Mom, I need to go." We hung up.

Once again, I was immediately stricken with that same deeply sickening feeling of dread. I said, "Bud, something has happened to someone in the family. I don't know who it is. It seems like it's someone far away, but it is someone who is very close to us."

We heard nothing from anyone that evening or night, but I felt zoned out for the rest of the day. Midmorning the next day, Jim called me. He said, "Mom, we just got back from the hospital. Yesterday, when we were talking, and I had to go, it was because Stefanie came out into the garage, crying. She had started to bleed. She lost the baby."

The unborn child was the family member I never had the chance to know—the baby who had instantly slipped so far away, to heaven. That was their second of two miscarriages before Stefanie got to the right doctor and gave birth to our beautiful baby girl, Jordan. Then, she had our precious baby boy—Peyton, middle name, O'Neal, after my brother, Jim. All thanks to God!

Evelyn, Billy, and I feel the same way about our children. They are the most important people in our lives. We raised them to know how much they are loved. We did not follow the paths of where we came from; instead, we created new ones, with a hope that the direction would be passed along to our children's children and so on.

CHAPTER 18

Melzar

Melzar dies in Tennesse, March 3, 1970

Jim was almost a year old in January 1970, when I accidently bumped into Melzar, my birth father, at Epps grocery store on Federal Road. I didn't recognize him. It had been dark when we last met in the parking lot at Carlton's. I had been afraid of him then, but now conversation seemed easier. He knew who I was, so he began to talk. He told me he lived up the street and pointed that direction. He and his friend were getting ready to go on a trip to Tennessee, to visit Uncle Grady and some other relatives. Once I felt more comfortable, I showed him a picture of Jim, who was at home with Bud.

He told me that he had a sewing machine to give me. We exchanged addresses and walked together to the parking lot. He had a great car, a 1967 Cougar, and he wanted to show it to me. The small-size Cougar was one of my favorites, and I bought one a year or so after that accidental meeting. Once again, our lives had crossed paths.

The next day, I went to work. When I got home, there was a new portable sewing machine sitting on my porch. I never learned how to sew a stitch, but later it came in handy as a trade-in on a new Kirby vacuum cleaner. The day after that, a redheaded woman came to my office to visit. She introduced herself as Nina and told me how happy Melzar was to have seen me and the picture of Jim. She was headed up the street to Todd's Shipyard, where he worked. Nina told me it was his birthday, and she was taking a cake for him to share with the crew. On her way, she decided to stop by my office to say hello.

When I was promoted to my then-current position at the company, I had access to all personnel files of past and present employees. I began to rearrange past employee records, to prepare them for placement in archives. I ran across one labeled "Barnes, Grady." I read where he had been the plant manager at Tenn-Tex, short for Tennessee-Texas. The company relocated from Tennessee to Texas many years earlier.

At that time, the file discovery was a surprise and struck me as odd. The initial *odd* feeling was about to be elevated to *bizarre* when I added everything up and realized: I had been separated from my birth family all my life. Now, all of a sudden, I discovered that I worked *and* lived practically next door to my father. Furthermore, of all the jobs in a big city like Houston, I ended up working for the same company that my uncle had once worked for. I associated with some of the same people he was friends with, walked the same hallways, and drank from the same water fountain, probably from the same coffeepot.

The old phrase "It's a small world" instantly took on a whole new meaning for me. A split second later, I realized the phrase itself was much too small a comparison. This had *nothing* to do with serendipity, coincidence, or chance. Something much larger was guiding my footsteps. This was nothing less than God Himself. I felt He was skillfully maneuvering the path I took and would take, while leaving choices I made and would make, entirely up to me. Would the path eventually bring me to a greater understanding?

I wanted to ask Nina questions like "How long have you two lived here? How are Aunt Doris and Johnny?" I thought of so many things but decided my father and I could discuss them in a more private setting at a later time, perhaps when he returned from his trip. Maybe then, I could get some answers from him—his perspective on how and why I ended up in Houston while my brothers had been raised together. Suddenly, it seemed as if he and I had so much to talk about, so much in common, so much to share. I looked forward to his return. I jotted down his birthday on my desk calendar, January 15, thanked Nina for coming, and for the sewing machine. I invited them to visit when they returned from their trip. She promised they would.

Finally, I would get some answers.

They were not able to keep that promise. Melzar died in Tennessee. At the time, I was told he died of a heart attack, but years later, I found out the truth. He was murdered. He lived on this earth for thirty-nine years, barely had turned forty, and he was gone. We didn't have much time to get to know one another, but I was glad for the few opportunities we had been given. Without them, I never would have been able to overcome some of my fear and negative feelings about him. He wouldn't have had the chance to follow through with his act of kindness, giving me the sewing machine. That simple act touched my heart. It let me know: On that day, my father thought about me.

I was thankful that our paths had crossed before he left. I knew we were placed in that grocery store on the same day at exactly the same time for a reason. I just didn't know how important and significant that reason was until later. It wasn't because I would never see him again, or that it was our last and final goodbye. It went beyond that. God opened the door and gave me the opportunity to show Melzar a picture of Jim, his only grandson. I chose to acknowledge their relationship by sharing my greatest gift with him in the form of a picture and a few spoken words.

There was a time when I could have been bitter and chosen not to have shown the picture to him. It's easy to forget our own mistakes and shortcomings: "for *all* have sinned and fall short of the glory of God" (Rom 3:23). Now, I could clearly see; I was the recipient of perhaps God's greatest gift. I was not bitter but glad that I had contributed to Melzar's happiness toward the end of his life. God opened that door and gave *me* a chance and a choice. He didn't want to leave me floundering around in all that ugly bitterness. He softened my heart, and I could see and understand what the ability to forgive could mean in one's life.

No one seemed to know many details about his death. He and Grady had gone to a local, Tennessee-Mississippi, borderline bar to shoot pool. Melzar liked to gamble. He won money, and apparently someone put something in his drink. He began to vomit—so much that he asphyxiated—and died there on the floor. Grady had only taken a few sips of his drink, but he got sick. Late that night or early the next morning, Melzar was found dead in his car. No money was found in his wallet or his pockets. Some people wanted to pursue an investigation but were warned not to.

I guess my father was another gambling victim. Could it have been the State Line Mob, perhaps the Dixie Mafia? It was probably just good ole boys. I don't know where Sheriff Bufford Pusser was; maybe it was his day off or maybe he was winding down in preparation of leaving the job, but I'm sure he could have handled the situation.

CHAPTER 19

Losses

The years passed quickly, and except for a few conversations with Gloria, I was out of the loop. In one of those conversations, she told me that Harold and Virginia had divorced, and since then, he met a wonderful girl, Carol. I didn't say so, but I was sort of glad. I recalled that his ex had not been very friendly. They seemed to be complete opposites. Harold is always friendly and kind to everyone. I couldn't figure out how the two of them ended up together in the first place. But we always hear that opposites attract. I guess that explained it.

Mother kept me busy. I always lived close to her, so I got the brunt of complaints to deal with and errands to run. She lived less than a mile from Tenn-Tex, where I had gone to work when Jim was only five weeks old. I often stopped to visit her on my way to work. Some mornings, I cooked breakfast for the two of us.

Mother enjoyed telling the other kids, "Vickie stops almost every day to see me." I thought she hoped it would encourage them to do the same, but all it did was create friction. One morning, she told Billy, again. He responded, "She's only doing that to get a free meal."

Of course, she told me what he said. She hoped to get a rise out of me. I know Billy knew better, and maybe he was joking, but more than likely he was fed up with the constant comparisons. We all were. She was very good at pitting one against the other, making one feel guilty at the expense of another. I now realize it was a form of manipulation, and sometimes it worked. She took every opportunity to berate our spouses and carried it on to our children. Once, she told Evelyn what a good basketball player Jim was, and made no comment about her son, Clay. They are the same age and sometimes played on the same or opposing teams. Or she would tell me how Clay would call her, just to talk, and wondered why Jim didn't. After all the years of comparison, we should have expected that, but it still hurt. Mother made no bones about it; she bluntly said what she thought and acted as if her straightforwardness (rudeness) was some sort of "gift." That being the case, my mother was truly "gifted." (I'm just thankful her gift did not include the power of "mother's intuition.")

Fortunately, our children did not take her nearly as seriously as we did. Maria was older than Jim, but both of them did odd jobs for Mother during the summer. They worked to earn money while they were out of school. When they were almost old enough, Mother told them to clean the roof of a house. Jim was to get on top of the roof and sweep it off while Maria stood below and bagged the pine needles, sticks, and leaves that he swept to the ground. It was a hard job for a couple of kids, but (mischievous) Jim was more than happy to cover Maria with roof debris.

After working hard most of the day, Mother took them to the cafeteria to eat dinner. They went through the line, and Maria picked out a scrumptious looking dessert, which she placed on her tray. She was about to sit down when Mother told her that she didn't need the dessert. She ordered her to return it and have the bill adjusted accordingly. Maria took it back, but she was extremely embarrassed. Jim thought it was pretty funny. He knew better than to get a dessert. He had returned several that he tried to slip by her. However, he wasn't laughing when Mother gave Maria ten dollars for helping out, and he received half as much. Mother told them that the pay, along with dinner (minus dessert), was a good wage. Jim, needless to say, was not happy with his reduced amount of pay, but he accepted it. He always had his own way of getting even.

Mother stopped by our house often. One day she entered, loudly singing the song she had just heard on the radio. She asked, "Jim, what's the first name of that Osborn boy who sings that song?"

Jim smiled and said, "Ozzy."

She said, "I'm going to stop at the store on my way home and pick up that tape."

Jim said, "Just ask them for the latest tape by Ozzy Osbourne. Here, I'll write the name down for you."

The singer of the song Mother liked so much was Donnie Osmond, but she never could remember names. "Dolly" was always Dolly Pard—close enough. If she could get somewhere in the ballpark, we could usually figure out who or what she was talking about. However, one time I was completely stumped. She sent me to the store to buy cat food. She said it was called "Little Bitty Spoonfuls of Tender Loving Care." I searched the cat *and* dog food aisles. It appeared the name she had given me was a combination of several products. It turned out that she wanted "Tender Vittles." That wasn't even close to the stadium.

It was years before I discovered Maria's first name was Rosa. When I called her house and asked for Maria, she would come to the phone and say, "Hi, Vickie."

One day I asked how she always knew it was me (that was long before Caller ID). She laughed and said, "Except for Alma, you're the only one who calls me Maria."

We were *all* young when I used to take Maria and Jim to Astroworld, a seventy-five-acre theme park (opened June 1968) located across the freeway from the Astrodome, "the Eighth Wonder of the World," which opened in April 1965. They were kids then, and I had lots of fun watching the two of them grow up. Astroworld has long since been gone, and the Dome is nothing more than a decaying heap of metal and memories with a bleak future existence.

Maria and I have remained very close throughout the years. She's more like a daughter to me. It's always nice to recall old times with someone who shares so many fun and special experiences. Regardless of some humiliating moments, Maria says that some of her favorite times are those spent with my mother. She always speaks fondly of her. And she doesn't mind, not one bit, that I still call her Maria.

Early one morning, Mother called to ask me to go with her to the nursing home to see my uncle. Apparently, someone called to report he was not doing well. Unckie had Parkinson's disease.

When we got there, he was propped up with pillows in a chair. There was a string of drool at his bottom lip, hanging on for dear life. His eyes looked tired and weak, so I sat directly in front of him, hoping he would recognize me, and we could talk. Mother went around in back of his chair. She said, "Look at him, Vickie. Just look at him. He's dying, just wasting away."

Tears began to stream down his face. I don't know what my mother expected of me, but I did know, Parkinson's or not, my uncle understood what she was saying.

I thought back about the person he had once been and recalled how close we seemed to be. I was somewhere between the ages of three and four when my birth father left me behind to live with them. I was six years old before there were any other children in the family. During those two and one-half to three years, Unckie took me everywhere with him.

We went grocery shopping together at Best Supermarket. The minute the door opened, someone would shout, "Shoot the sherbet to me, Herbert." There would be laughter, and someone would comment about him "bringing his little helper with him." The grocery store was in a strip center located across the street, adjacent to Daddy's store on Market Street. Market Street and Federal Road were the two major hubs of Greens Bayou. Almost anything anyone might need could be found at a business in one of those two locations. The Greens Bayou Pharmacy, otherwise known as "Rexall Drug Store," owned by Mr. Bob, was right next door to the supermarket. The drugstore is where my uncle would sometimes buy a box of Pangburn's cream-filled chocolates wrapped in thick, shiny, slick white wrapping paper. He let me choose the color of the pretty pastel ribbon or bow. We would take them home to surprise Grandma. My uncle made me feel special. I felt like the single chocolate wrapped in gold foil in Grandma's box of candy.

The Grand Theater, a freestanding building, stood next to the strip center. I could stand at the glass window of Daddy's store, drink my small bottled Coke with a salty package of Tom's peanuts "tumped" inside it, look across the street, and see what was playing at the picture show. It only cost twenty-five cents to see two movies, a cartoon, and a newsreel. The newsreel told us what was going on in the world or was a short documentary on something that *had* gone on. What was the point? In either case, it was too late to do anything about whatever it was. I loved the cartoon, but I could do without the minihistory lesson. I thought it would be great to work at the Grand Theater. I loved the idea of scooping popcorn into the red and white striped paper sacks, getting ice, and drawing soda pop out of the dispenser into the matching red and white cups.

My uncle used to bring Hershey bars or roasted peanuts home to me. He bought the peanuts from a street vendor who was disabled. He had some sort of peanut heater hooked up to his cart. I can still taste them, always hot and fresh.

One day, we were in my uncle's old truck, a 1949 Ford, when we stopped at an icehouse. He gave me a dime to buy some penny candy and Bazooka Joe bubble gum. I always preferred it over Double Bubble because it had the comic strip. To this day, I don't know what possessed me, but when we got back into the truck to leave, I leaned against the door and pulled the handle straight up. I almost fell out onto the street, but he grabbed me just in time. It scared him to death.

He was always partial to me and gave me lots of attention when I was little. That was something I never had received from any man. My own father had gone away and left me behind.

Pic showing Daddy's store, Ray's Auto Parts, connected to Fain's
Auto Repair, two long-standing community businesses

I have read books on the subject of overcoming rejection and how to deal with the devastating feelings it can create. In my research, I learned about the importance of a daughter feeling loved and valued by her father, the first and most important man in her life. He is the person who sets the standard of how she will expect other males to treat her. It is the father who can instill confidence and make the child feel secure and valued. It is also the father who has the power to keep those positive feelings withheld from the child's life.

I think it is just as important for a son to feel loved and valued by his father. In some ways, it might even be more crucial. Perhaps it could be the answer to how we break the ongoing, unacceptable cycle of males abandoning their families. The teachings of a father committed to family values would set the standard of how a son should treat his family. We often hear, "These days, there are so many children being raised in a one-parent family; almost always, it is the mother."

How are "these days" any different from the 1940s and '50s? When people talk about "the good ole days" or reference "when men were men," I don't see a lot of difference between then and now. There were four children in my "adopted" family. Each of us had different birth parents, and each one of us was initially abandoned by the first man in our life—our father.

My adopted father, while a good man, worked all the time. He was a workaholic who had little spare time. I rarely saw him, except on Sundays, but I am so thankful for those Sundays. The store was open Monday through Saturday. Occasionally, I would ride downtown with him to pick up auto parts. Sometimes, I made sandwiches at home, wrapped them in wax paper, pinned the wrapping with a toothpick, and took them to the store for Daddy's lunch.

My mother always told us kids that Unckie was a "reformed alcoholic." I do remember a few times when he slipped. Mother lashed out at him. Those times frightened me. She threatened that if he drank one more time; he would have to leave and could never come back. I worried about where he would go. Where could he live? I was just a little girl, but Mother told me many times my own birth father was an alcoholic. She said I could never drink because I had "alcoholism in my genes." I had no idea what she meant, but I didn't have any place to go if she made me leave, so I refused to wear *jeans* for years. While my uncle's impropriety made her mad, I think it gave her a sense of being needed. He was broken, he needed fixing, and she was just the person who could "fix" him.

Now, here he was, slumped way down in a big aqua plastic chair that seemed to be swallowing him, a little at a time. He was beyond any fixing, truly wasting away in a nursing home. He was almost unrecognizable, a shell of the man he struggled to be. He passed away within the year. I asked the pastor to include in his eulogy that we never heard him say an unkind word about anyone. He did.

Daddy was seventy-six years old when he passed away in 1976. He had been diagnosed with leukemia eight years earlier, but as long as he stayed under the doctor's care and went in for regular transfusions, he did well. It seems strange to say, but one of his hospital stays was one of the best memories I have of time spent with my father.

Daddy had become weak, and his blood count was off. He had to go into the hospital for a transfusion. At the same time, I became ill. The doctor put me into the same hospital to run tests. Daddy and I spent a lot of time together, playing checkers and cards. I will never forget the fun we had, and how, by some strange, miraculous coincidence, we were there to entertain one another during that hospital stay. Daddy had never taken that much time off work, and we made the most of what could have been a poor set of circumstances.

It was not until I returned home from the hospital that my test results were received. That year, lots of people had contracted hepatitis from eating contaminated oysters. I was one of them. Needless to say, I was not very popular at my job. A medical bus and staff were sent out to the work site. Everyone in the office and the plant had to be inoculated. It wasn't that the injection was so bad, but each person had to be weighed because the medicine dispensed was based on a person's weight. The scale was in an open area, and the women didn't care nearly as much about getting the disease as they did about the public weigh-in. Fortunately, Daddy didn't acquire the illness, probably because of all that clean blood he was receiving by transfusion.

One Saturday, several months after our joint hospital stay, my dad was in the top of a tree, trimming limbs. He was a picture of health. Within a couple of days, it became difficult for him to breathe. Mother and I took him to the hospital, where he was diagnosed with pneumonia. He died there, fighting for his last breath of air. I was in the room when the nurses and doctors began to violently pound his chest, even breaking ribs, in a failed attempt to resuscitate him. That is a scene that haunts me to this day.

Jim was eight years old when Daddy died. He took Papaw's death very hard. When Jim was a baby, Daddy would come by our house every Sunday morning on his way to church. It was the only day of the week you would see him wearing anything besides his dark gray work uniform—gray pants and gray shirt with the name Ray's Auto Parts stitched in white above the shirt pocket. On Sundays, he always wore a suit, white shirt, and tie. He stopped at our house to have coffee or breakfast, but mostly, he came to see Jim.

I regretfully look back at those Sunday mornings when I grumbled to myself about how difficult it was to climb out of bed and answer an early-morning doorbell. It seemed like we would just get to sleep when that bell, like some obnoxious alarm clock, would ring. Of course, that woke the baby up, but *he* would be smiling ear to ear when Papaw appeared in his doorway. His battery was fully charged, and he was ready to play.

In my own defense, I usually had just gotten to sleep. Jim was one of those babies who did not require much rest. He slept so lightly that a singing canary could wake him up, crying and demanding one more bottle. If there is anything good about aging, it is that we get a little wiser. I now realize the value of time spent with our loved ones. It is, as they say, priceless. Sometimes, on those Sunday mornings, Daddy took Jim to church with him. They had been close.

I was still working at Tenn-Tex that July 1976, when Daddy passed away. I had to go into the office to prepare the company's quarterly tax reports, due by the end of the month. My coworkers were sympathetic and tried to comfort me by encouraging conversation. I began to share growing up stories with them, and we all laughed. Suddenly, my laughter turned into an outburst of tears. I could not stop crying. I always heard, "You know that a person is crazy when he laughs and cries at the same time." Years later, I think I realized the reason behind the simultaneous emotions, when I first heard the song "The Greatest Man I Never Knew."

For many of us working women, our coworkers become such an integral part of our lives. After all, we spend more awake time with them than with our own families. We get to know one another on so many different levels. There were three of us girls working in the office at Tenn-Tex Alloy. Nelda was in the front office. She was the receptionist and payroll clerk for the hourly personnel (about 120 men at full capacity), and Gloria was the shipping clerk. She was responsible for billing and keeping inventory records. The three of us have remained friends throughout the years. We don't get together much anymore, but we still talk on the phone. If any one of us needs something, the other two will rise to the occasion. That's just the kind of bond we developed during our years of working together at (what we refer to as) the "greatest job we could have ever had." We were all young then, and we watched each other's children grow up. We did a lot of growing up too. We shared secrets, laughter, and tears.

Once, when we needed to hire an additional person, we made sure it would be somebody who would fit in.

That person was Jane. She had three children at home and was very witty and intelligent. She fit like a glove, and the three of us became four. Occasionally, the four of us would get together after work, for dinner. Jane liked mint juleps. She fancied herself in a rocking chair on the big white porch of a southern plantation home, sipping mint juleps and eating bonbons, with Sneaky, her cat, on her lap.

It was happy hour, and the waitress brought Jane two strong, deep-green drinks. I guess she began to feel a little frisky after the first minty treat because when she downed the second, she blurted out, "Bring on the cat!" I couldn't help but think about the little cartoon mouse hiding in the champagne glass. (Hiccup!)

Meanwhile, in the background, Kenny Rogers was belting out the words: "You picked a fine time to leave me, Lucille, with four hungry children and a crop in the field." I guess the bourbon (and lack of dinner) got to Jane, because she raised her glass to toast Lucille, and (an octave beyond loud) said, "I think she picked a helluva good time to leave!" Gloria, Nelda, (some people who we didn't know), and I laughed until we cried.

One day I was working in my office when Jane came in looking worried and pale. She had been to the doctor that morning, and now she was receiving some disturbing news. The doctor's office had called back and needed her to take test results to Rosewood Hospital, immediately. She was so shaken by the request that she was unable to drive. I asked permission to take her to the hospital, and we were on our way. The hospital was on the other side of town. I had no idea how to get there, but between the two of us, we managed to find it. We took the results inside and returned to the car to leave. My battery was dead. We walked to a nearby gas station. A man who worked there came to help us. He charged fifty dollars to jump start the car.

The next day, the doctor requested that Jane's husband take her back to the hospital. Things began to happen so fast that it all seemed like a blur. Jane called me to say she had been diagnosed with cervical cancer, stage four. The doctor told her she could choose to go to M. D. Anderson, where he said she would be a number, or stay there for treatments. I hoped she would go to MDA but decided it best not to voice my opinion. Everyone knew of M. D. Anderson's good reputation, but in the late '70s, the very thought of a cancer hospital scared most people to death. Jane began the treatment process at Rosewood. She continued to work part time. After each treatment, she became weaker, until she could no longer work.

She wasn't able to eat much. I would try to be encouraging by taking food to her. I told her we could still have lunch together at her house. We did, almost every day. I recall her saying, "I've lost so much weight. If I could just get rid of the cancer, I would be in great shape."

I also took a book, *The Power of Positive Thinking*. We read from it often. She told me her old friends rarely came to see her. She understood they no longer knew what to say. I didn't say so, but I certainly could understand. No matter how close two people are, it is even difficult to write words of inspiration to a terminally ill person. A "Get well" card seems ludicrous.

One day, Jane called me at work, mentioned what a beautiful day it was, and said she wished she was at Galveston walking in the waves. I had vacation time due, so I left the office to pick her up. I feel so blessed that I was given the opportunity to replace words with action. There's nothing more invigorating than those spur-of-the-moment, spontaneous little trips.

When we got to the beach, we took off our shoes, rolled our pants legs up, and walked—hand in hand—out into those big rolling waves, as far as we could go. We witnessed the artistic hand of God in the subtle beauty of a sunset. We didn't say a word. Our spirits were calm—and for a moment, total peace was found there. God's grace flowed down and covered both of us. I think the late Dr. Maya Angelou's words "Life is not measured by the number of breaths we take, but by the moments that take our breath away" were written for such a time as that.

Jane passed away that year. The loss was unbearable, and I couldn't talk about it, or her, for years. I made a decision right then and there: "I will never allow myself to get that close to anyone again in my life."

Since I associate people and circumstances with music, the one song that always reminds me of Jane is "Blue Eyes Crying in the Rain." Jane had pretty blonde hair—the reflection of sunshine. She had beautiful blue eyes, which filled with tears when she spoke on the dark subject of having to leave her children so soon. She had a loving heart and a bright, joyful spirit. She was my friend.

Union Carbide leased Tenn-Tex Alloy, and by 1980, plans were made to shut down our small company. All hourly and salaried employees were laid off or terminated except the president, Jim Hays; vice president, Roland Loewen; shipping supervisor, James Strickland; and me. I was asked to stay for the purpose of closing out the accounting books. That was a difficult time. It had such a negative emotional and financial impact on so many families, so many lives. The closeness of its people was truly a brotherhood and sisterhood in every sense of the word.

Union Carbide blamed the demise of the company on strikes and the demands of our union men, the United Steelworkers Local 214. I personally felt its slow death began on the day the lease-purchase agreement was signed. I think Carbide wanted to eliminate the little man and do away with the competition. I saw the writing on the wall and began to watch the job ads. One day, I saw an ad in the newspaper for a bookkeeper at a local law firm. I responded with my resume and was called to interview. I accepted the job, with an understanding: I could only work Mondays through Thursdays. Fridays had to be reserved for paperwork at Tenn-Tex. That routine lasted well over a year.

As I pulled out of the Tenn-Tex Alloy Corporation of Houston parking lot for the last time, I stopped to look back with deep sadness. One time, a great man told me, "Don't look back. Looking back means you want to live in the past." At that moment, that is exactly what I wanted to do.

I visualized the plant when it was alive. The three furnaces seemed to have a life of their own. Strong, muscular men fired the furnaces and fed their ravenous appetites while the savage beasts burned furiously. They had to get more production. The mixture had to be right. Nobody wanted their big, boiling, bellies to blow. There was always the chance that the "Tri-Monster" could take a human life. That had happened before.

There was a brief warning. It started with a deep, distressful rumble, which turned into a groan. Rapidly, the rumbling and groaning increased to an uncontrollable roar. The roar grew louder—then—*louder.* The ground beneath us began to vibrate and shake. It sounded and felt as if it was some gigantic pressure cooker filled with suppressed, pent-up rage—capable of total devastation. Suddenly, there was a tremendous explosion! The monstrously violent eruption was followed by the alarming sound of shattered glass. The contemptible catastrophe created confusion and chaos. It left us trembling with fear and anger. One of our fine men lay still and lifeless on that horrific path of destruction.

Now, there it stood, cold and lifeless, beyond resurrection, like its sister, Armco (Sheffield Steel), across the street. She had long since been quieted. Monopolizing utility giant Houston Lighting and Power probably mourned the loss as much as any outsider could. The plug had been pulled—the meter suspended—on this Houston, Texas, industry. Although they were paid plenty in fines, regulatory giants Harris County Pollution Control and the Environmental Protection Agency were, more than likely, deliriously ecstatic that neither plant released so much as a puff. They had "ceased their fearless roar."

As I pulled away, Simon and Garfunkel were singing "The Sound of Silence" on the radio. That time, I didn't look back.

CHAPTER 20

The Trip

My work at the law firm was not nearly as stressful as my prior job had been. I had no Great Oz up in New York to report to every month. The attorneys were easy to work for. I liked them, and I loved my new job. Although the firm's name was Gray, Roche, and Burch, Mr. Burch had purchased the business from Frank Gray a few years prior to my employment. In fact, Mr. Gray was working at another building but continued to maintain his association with our firm. That worked out well for everybody. Mr. Gray had been practicing law in the east end of Houston for decades. He was a well-known, well-respected attorney and former judge.

My mother was one of his first clients, and I learned that he had handled the adoption of my brother, Billy. As was my previous job, the firm was in close proximity to my mother's home. While she would never have gone to the alloy plant, she felt free to drop in anytime at the firm. And later, when Mr. Gray relocated to our offices, that's just what she did. Mother came anytime and many times. Lots of those visits were to change her will. The will changed each time she got upset with one of her kids. It was changed, and changed often. If an award was given for the thickest will file in the history of our firm, Mother would have won it, hands down.

In December 1979, Irene Gray, Mr. Gray's wife, decided to have the firm's Christmas party at his other location. I had never been there and had never met his new secretary, Judy. I took my plate of food and sat down across from her desk. We began to talk. I felt like I had known her for years, and we just *clicked*. She made me laugh, and I said she "missed her calling." I thought she should be a stand-up comedian because she was so funny. She said, "You should meet my sisters, Bett and Iris." I have. She's right. When the three of those girls get together, they create an entire evening of entertainment. Their stories are one comedy episode after another, which could become a never-ending, award-winning series. That was the first day of what has become my lifelong friendship with Judy. I've always heard, "When one door closes, He opens another."

Meeting Judy and her family has been proof that what I heard is true.

No one could ever replace Jane—my memory of her is forever tucked away deep inside my heart. Judy brought me out of the depths of sorrow, and our friendship represented a new beginning. It is still vibrant and alive as it serves to enrich and enhance my life every day.

After the Christmas and New Year holidays, Mr. Gray and Judy moved to the Federal Road office with us. What a great day that was. That evening after work, I was in the parking lot when I couldn't help but notice a familiar-looking car parked there. It was a burnt-orange or copper-color Chevy Caprice, with a beige vinyl top and beige interior. I never knew but one other person who drove the exact same car, my late friend, Jane. Seeing it brought back a multitude of memories. The next day, I discovered the car belonged to Judy. It felt like confirmation or approval, perhaps something bigger than that, in the great scheme of things.

In the summer of 1986, Judy agreed to go with me to Memphis, Tennessee. We were to meet Gloria and Dale there. They were driving from Lansing, and we were flying from Texas. About a half-hour into the flight, I began to worry about whether they would recognize me or if I would know either of them. It had been almost twenty years since Jim's death, when we last saw one another.

I described both (as I remembered) to Judy and asked her to help me locate them when we landed. This reminded me of a book I read to my son, Jim, when he was little: *Are You My Mother?* It is a story about a baby bird that hatches when its mother is away from her nest. The little bird falls from the nest and begins to search for her. The baby bird asks everyone he meets, including a dog and a cat, "Are you my mother?" It all worked out fine for the little bird. I dozed off, feeling sure it would work out for me.

We exited the plane, still full of anxiety, but soon realized we didn't have to worry about recognizing anyone. Judy nudged me when she saw a dark-haired woman practically running in my direction. A short, chunky, slightly balding man was trying to keep up with her.

Judy stood back and watched as a mother and daughter reunited after twenty years. Gloria and I hugged one another and then took a moment to really look into each other's eyes. It was an emotional event, and I couldn't help but cry. I looked at Judy and noticed her wipe a few tears from her eyes as well. The tears shed at the airport were the beginning of many during the trip. Not all of them would be tears of sorrow—however; each and every one would contribute to making it a trip to remember for a lifetime.

Introductions were made, and we left the airport to have lunch and go sightseeing around Memphis. We went to the famous Peabody Hotel and visited the ducks on the roof. We listened to jazz and rode in a horse-drawn carriage on Beale Street. It was a lively and great place to be in the summer of '86. Later that afternoon, we ended up at Dale's sister's house in Germantown, a suburb of Memphis. Charlie and Norma (pronounced Chaaalie and Knome in Tennessean) were the ultimate host and hostess. We appreciated them opening their home to us, two virtual strangers.

Gloria wanted to take us on a road trip to visit relatives, Jim's grave, and eventually Nashville. We were both excited about the prospect of seeing Nashville, and I was looking forward to going to the cemetery, since I had never seen where Jim was buried. On the morning we were to leave, Judy and I woke up at the crack of dawn, ready and rarin' to go. Gloria, however, basked in the fact that her daughter was there, and she took her sweet time, savoring every moment. Judy and I walked the sidewalk like a couple of teenagers impatiently waiting on our late dates to take us somewhere, anywhere. Finally, with every hair in place, perfect makeup, jewelry on board, and dressed to the nines, Gloria was ready to leave.

A few hours later, we arrived at Archie and Vinnie's home. The two of them were sitting on the front porch of the old shotgun-style house. I could tell by the smiles on their faces that they were expecting us. Gloria hesitated for a moment. I felt sure she was recalling childhood memories from her years of growing up there. She opened the door and got out of the car, then walked to my door and opened it for me. She extended her left hand to help me out. I exited the car and stood beside her. She looked so proud, standing there with me—her child, the little girl who had been taken in the middle of the night from this same house, thirty-five years earlier. She was so excited to present a grown-up daughter to her own aunt and uncle, the two people who raised her.

I wondered how many times she had prayed for this moment—had mentally lived out this scene. I felt just like that little ten-year-old girl again. The one whose mother came to visit her in Houston, and the loving way she looked at her daughter made the child feel so special. Now, thirty years later, it occurred to me that I had worried needlessly back then. A child will never outgrow a need for his or her mother.

Our next stop was to visit Archie and Vinnie's twin daughters. When we entered the living room, I saw a picture of a younger Geraldine or Lurline and commented about how much we favored. It was strange to see people who looked like me. One of the girls told a story about the last time they saw me, when I was three years old. She is the one who told me how I begged her to pin curl my hair and how for years she had regretted not doing so. "Because" she said, "we didn't know that was the last time we would ever see you."

We left Chewalla and headed for Martin, Tennessee, to the cemetery. I guess meeting all those people from my past dredged up old questions. I asked Gloria how I ended up in Houston with my mother and daddy, the Faulkner's. The answer was painful. She told me what she had heard: Melzar had sold me for a certain amount of money. I asked her, "How much?" I wondered what the price of a child was. Also, I wondered if this could have something to do with the "magic words" his brother, J. B., had used to help Gloria gain entrance to see me, back when I was only ten years old. I had always wondered about those words. She replied that she heard the amount was $10,000. I guessed that was a good price back in 1951. Bud and I had only paid $9,250 for our first house in 1969. I would have figured *that* much money could have bought lots of kids. Suddenly, I had a flashback—a picture of three-year-old me, standing with my birth father next to a brand new convertible with the top down. After all, he *did* love cars. With that much money, he could have bought the car and got change back. Maybe he could have bought a car lot.

After that, I wasn't nearly so eager to ask any more questions. In fact, dealing with the answer was harder than I could have imagined. I cried, on and off, all the way to Martin. Judy said I rode huddled in the corner, next to the left back door. My back was turned to everyone. I didn't remember. All I could remember was the feeling of pain and humiliation that came with having been bought and paid for. What kind of parent could sell their child?

Toward the end of the trip to Martin, I guess Dale was getting tired. He veered off the pavement and ran over some speed bumps. The bumpy ride and loud noise startled Gloria out of a sound sleep. She came alive like a boxer out of her corner when the bell rings. With flailing arms, she screamed, "Shit, Dale, what's wrong?"

"Oh, it wasn't anything; just ran over a little bump in the road."

We made a much-needed stop at Walmart. I purchased flowers to place on Jim's grave.

We arrived in Martin, Tennessee, at dusk. It was my first time to see the cemetery. I observed the pretty surroundings with large trees that shaded the area. *What a lovely resting place—so quiet and peaceful.* I lingered there, alone for a while. I couldn't help but think about the injustice of the missed opportunity to get to know my brother. I felt cheated. We had only seen each other one time that I could remember, and had only spoken on the phone once. It certainly wasn't our fault. Someone was to blame—not us; we were just kids. I placed the flowers on his grave and then stood at the site and wept. After a while, I returned to the car where everyone was patiently waiting for me.

Gloria decided that Dale should drive on to Nashville. It was already about six in the evening and had been an emotionally draining day, but Gloria wanted to go; so we drove, and we drove.

I guess the hum of Gloria's soft gentle snore (with her occasional snort) must have lulled us all to sleep. All of us, that is, except Judy, who was sitting in the back, behind the passenger seat, saying, "Vickie, wake up." Dale had begun to drift off, and so had the car. Judy's voice became increasingly louder as she repeated, "Dale—Dale—Dale!" Judy nudged me at about the same time the car crossed over the center line toward oncoming traffic and then veered off down a steep, football-field-sized rocky embankment.

Dale's eyes were now wide open and peering straight ahead. He desperately held on, clenching both sides of the steering wheel as we came within inches of a huge satellite dish on our right and barely missed thirty-foot pine trees on our left, all the while bouncing up and down over the rocks. It felt like we were test-riding in a human-sized blender, but I tell you, Dale handled that car like a bronco-ridin' cowboy tames a wild stallion. Ye-haw! Finally, we came to a skidding stop under the portico of a Quality Inn. We Texas girls were rightfully impressed. Meanwhile, Gloria was in constant scream mode, screeching, "Shit, Dale, are you trying to kill us all?"

We looked in the plate glass window to see three awestruck men who obviously witnessed our descent from the other side of the highway. I halfway expected all of them to hold up cards with a "10" marked on each one. Instead, they just stood there, staring at us. I swear I could hear the theme song from *Deliverance*, "Battle of the Banjos," playing in my head.

Dale got out of the car, looked in the side mirror (which miraculously was still attached), and smoothed his sparse hair.

Gloria remained in the car and rotated her wig by the light of the vanity mirror. She turned to look at us and asked (in the sweetest voice she could possibly muster up), "Would you girls like to go in?"

Obviously still shaken, Judy replied, "Not *no* but *hell no*! I'm not getting out of this car with those people already thinking we are a couple of old-maid, middle-aged, redheaded, retarded daughters on vacation with their parents!"

I asked her, "Why retarded?"

She said, "Well, shit, Dale, look at our parents!"

Gloria and I both laughed until we cried.

Dale came back to report, "No rooms between here and Nashville 'cause it's Fanfare week, when all the stars are there." Gloria heard the word *stars*. I saw her inhale a quick breath. With dreamy eyes, raised eyebrows, and a cat that ate the canary grin, she turned and looked back to see if we had heard, and if we shared, her enthusiasm. We didn't.

Judy offered to drive, but Dale said he had everything under control. We drove on to Nashville where there were *still* no rooms (Nashville + Fanfare week = no rooms). Go figure. It was three in the morning when Gloria suddenly remembered a relative who lived in Nashville. She was a cousin whom Gloria hadn't seen or spoken with in over eleven years. Now, if she could only remember her last name.

We found a phone booth, complete with telephone and phone book. Gloria called the long-lost cousin. The lady graciously got up out of bed and came to meet us so we could follow her back to her home. She explained that she was remodeling the basement apartment, which was not yet complete. However, there was a comfortable bed with clean linen. It sounded like the Taj Mahal to Judy and me.

It was at least four in the morning, and we had just gone to bed when there was a soft knock on our door. The door opened; Gloria made a Loretta Young grand entrance into the room, swirling around at the bottom stair. She was wearing her long, lavender, beautifully flowing silk peignoir, along with one of her many, multicolored, terry cloth turban head wraps to match. With her head held high, she sniffed at the air and arrogantly said, "I can't *believe* she put you girls down here with this mildew smell." She walked around the room, swiping furniture for dust particles with her index finger, while stating, "She's always been *Ms. Hoity Toity.*" The only thing missing was the white glove. She was acting like the spoiled rich kid you would never invite to a slumber party. We didn't say a word, but we both yawned, and she went back upstairs. I guessed she was just tired and, like any other child, she was acting out. Or maybe the head wrap was too tight.

The next morning, our hostess had prepared homemade biscuits with her own watermelon rind jelly, bacon, and sausage. All were served on beautiful china. Once again, she apologized for the room having been unfinished. We let her know how much we appreciated all of the hospitality, and apologized for barging in on her in the wee hours of the morning. We discovered, just that morning, the poor lady was still grieving. Her husband had passed away only a month or so earlier.

Later on, we repacked the car and left for Opryland. The only "star" we saw was Mary Ann Gordon, and that was purely by accident. At a restaurant where we were eating, Judy spotted a pretty lady with her son. She mentioned that she recognized her as Kenny Rogers's wife. Judy said, "Mary Ann used to be on the TV series *Hee Haw.*"

Gloria overheard. We watched her jump up from the table, hurry over to the lady, and ask, "Are you Kenny Rogers'ess wife?" I'm sure Mary Ann thought we were straight from "Kornfield Kounty." *Salute!*

Before we left Opryland, I bought a T-shirt for Bud. It read as if it was custom made for him. He wore it for years. The catchy saying on front was "First it's one thing; then it's your mother."

Since our return from "the Trip," "Shit, Dale!" has continued to be a catchphrase among Judy's and her sister's families. Like a typical bad habit, it caught on in our Bunko group, although the ladies weren't sure where it came from. A bad roll of the dice would often bring out the colorful phrase. They said the two words seemed to go together; they just rolled off the tongue and adequately expressed sudden disappointment and frustration with their poor bunko performance. Enough said. The meaning was self-explanatory.

CHAPTER 21

The Collector

I know the big house must have felt empty. Grandma passed away years earlier, in 1967. She was ninety-two. By the end of that year, the children were married with extended families of their own. Less than ten years later, both my uncle and my daddy were gone.

I think it was Mother's loneliness or perhaps the lack of having anyone or anything to control, which made her become a *collector* of dogs. She had three house dogs and at least that many in the yard, maybe lots more. There were several enclosures on the property, and I think she stashed them around in undisclosed areas. The dogs became an obsession. She no longer seemed to care about her yard or the beautiful roses she planted.

She quit going to their vacation home in the Hill Country, and it ran down. At one time, she and Daddy loved the country fresh air and getting away. The house sat unattended for years. We didn't know when someone stripped it of copper wiring. They probably sold it for a few cents on the dollar. She had the wiring replaced but had no desire to go.

At different times, we kids would suggest having family get-togethers. We thought it would be fun to stay at the house some summer weekends, but she didn't want to leave her dogs. Furthermore, Mother didn't want any of us to stay in the house if she wasn't going to be there. She used to say, "You might forget to turn the water off when you leave," as one excuse for not wanting us to go. We never knew the real reasons. We finally quit asking. If we did go, we rented a cabin on the lake.

During her *dog collector* years, Mother developed breast cancer. She had to have a complete mastectomy. Mother was tough. She said she was ready to go home the same night as her surgery.

The doctor asked about her living conditions. He said, "Mrs. Faulkner must be in a sterile environment before she can be released to go home."

He didn't realize the words *sterile* and *home* couldn't be used in the same sentence when speaking of Mother's house.

I passed the word on to Billy and his wife. Evelyn lived out of town but planned to spend the next day at the hospital with Mother. We took that opportunity to go to her house and try to decontaminate it. We had one day to do a month's job: clean two rooms.

First, the guys cleaned out the carport. If it was raining she would be able to drive to the side door and walk directly into the house without getting wet. That was no easy job. Mother (with all that rent property) had become a hoarder. Renters left things. She kept them. She wouldn't throw anything away. All the stuff stacked up over the years.

While they worked on that project, we girls cleaned her bathroom and the master bedroom, where no one had slept in years. That doesn't sound like a lot of work, and ordinarily it wouldn't have been a big task, but at Mother's house, it was colossal. I phoned Mother at the hospital and spoke with Evelyn to let her know *why* (doctor's orders) and *what* we were trying to do. Mother had a conniption fit. She told Evelyn we "had no business being there," and she "bet we were throwing away or stealing her valuables."

I assured her the only thing we had thrown away were some old, dirty, faded, plastic flowers that had been lying around in the house or under the carport. You would have thought we had thrown away her wedding pictures. Those plastic flowers were invaluable. She had so many plans for their use. We were extremely disheartened and certainly unappreciated, but we pressed on, and by late that night we had those rooms sterile and patient-ready. Mother could be released to go home.

Mother's drain tubes had to be measured and emptied twice a day. Since I worked up the street, I did the job on my lunch break and after work. I didn't mind. She acted nice to me while I was there, but when she talked to Evelyn, the rest of us (outcasts) were still known as *thieves*. It took Mother a long time to get over the loss of those plastic flowers (not both breasts).

When the last dog died of old age, (and was found under her bed after a week of MIA) we felt a great sense of relief. We were in hopes that she might have some incentive to get her act together and her house cleaned up. Evelyn and I volunteered to help, but Mother declined the offer. (Probably afraid we might find some more plastic flowers to steal.)

It wasn't long before a bad situation became worse. Mother became a *cat collector*. She had a renter who moved out and left behind, inside the apartment, a mother cat with several kittens. Mother, ever the rescuer with a need to be needed, took the cat and kittens home with her. I couldn't blame her. I felt her love for animals was one of her endearing qualities. I should have known she would become obsessed again; first it was people, then dogs, and now cats. She fed the orphaned cat and kittens outside, and it wasn't long before six became twelve.

She had her "Special Kitties." She kept those inside with her. Her two favorites were Doty or Toby (they were twins, and I don't think she knew who was who) and Felix. Many times she asked me to *promise* I would take Felix and Doty (or Toby) if anything should happen to her. I would answer her truthfully. I reminded her that I had two cats, and Bud wouldn't allow me to have them. All of Mother's cats were named and well taken care of. She took all of them to the vet and had them "fixed," but that didn't stop people from bringing them to her, even placing them in her car. By this time, she had developed a reputation and a name—Cat Lady.

I never knew a cat that didn't know what a litter box was, until I met some of Mother's "Special Kitties." We tried our best to get her to take some of them to the SPCA, even offered to do it for her, but she wouldn't hear of it. She became extremely upset when we suggested such a terrible thing. I am a *cat person,* but there is a limit! I made countless trips to the grocery store for litter and cat food.

Evelyn doesn't like cats, Billy doesn't like them, plus he has a cat allergy, but Mother got mad and couldn't understand why she had few visitors. There was never a place to sit, and if there was, it was covered with hair or worse. (Yes, much worse!) It broke our hearts to see the house and the way Mother lived. She was in total denial of her situation. She said, "My house is not dirty; it's just cluttered." She made sure *we* felt guilty about not visiting more often. When we called to ask how she was doing, her response was "I'm just over here all alone and dying."

The living room she had once been so proud of was hardly livable. The furniture we had once put gallons of wax on was used for scratching posts. The cats ruined the vinyl top on her Cadillac parked in the garage. This was a far cry from my memory of Mother and Daddy proudly sitting in our beautiful living room with the owner of a Pontiac or Buick dealership, ordering and paying cash for a new car, which he would personally deliver to their home. We tried to talk her into hiring some help to clean. She wouldn't hear of it. She didn't want other people in her house, going through her things.

At that time, Mother was still able to drive and meet friends for lunch at the I-10 East Luby's Cafeteria. My sister was working downtown, and it wasn't too far for me to travel, so we occasionally met Mother and her friends there. They went almost daily and always sat in the back left corner booth. We knew where to find them. Mother's favorite tea server, Maria, (her real name was probably Rosa) once told me affectionately, "They come in almost every day. I call them my Ladies in the Corner."

One day, I was going to surprise her and show up for lunch. I was headed to the back (with my tray) to join them and was stricken with an overwhelming sense of grief. As I approached the table, I looked up to really see each one of them, as if for the first time; one had her walker; one a cane; all with their hair freshly fixed; all in their wrinkle-free; polyester tops (long since outdated); and all with smiles, because today they had the company of one another. But age was knocking on the door and threatening their very existence. I visualized the inevitable, one empty space at a time. I could hardly bear the painful thought of losing them, let alone the thought of them losing each other, or being the only one left behind. I had to stop, unroll my silverware, and use my cloth napkin to wipe the tears from my eyes before I could go any farther. That day, reality slapped me directly in the face.

Mother was the one left behind. The others either passed away or lost a spouse, which caused them to move away, closer to remaining family members. Mother didn't seem to regret her inability to drive to Luby's anymore. Evelyn or I took her there weekly for lunch. She had a few near misses in the car and became a little skeptical of driving. In a way, that was a good thing. Evelyn and I dreaded the day "she" would have to tell her, "No more driving." We knew Mother would make us regret it, but we were extremely concerned about her getting behind the wheel. Most anyone (with any sense at all) would not want to be on the road between Miles Street and Uvalde Road or Miles Street and Federal Road when she was on the loose.

One day, my son's close friend, Jimmy, saw her driving the wrong way up Uvalde. She was traveling north in the southbound lane. He pulled his car in front of hers, blocking oncoming traffic, until she could get turned around to go the right way. Another time, she was driving west on the feeder road toward Uvalde and decided to pull into the gas station on the corner. She waited on the car in front of her to fill up and move away from the pump. When the car moved, she accelerated and quickly discovered she had inadvertently put her car in reverse, causing it to back out into the fast-moving, oncoming traffic of the feeder road. A truck driver in an eighteen-wheeler blocked for her that day. I guess the real reason she put up no fight and actually said, "I think I might need to stop driving" was when she pulled out of a U-Haul parking lot, crossed over the white line (she said both of them had crossed the line), and scraped her car all the way down one side, from the headlight to the trunk. It's a good thing every vehicle she drove was really large, similar to a parade float. She wouldn't tell me about the incident because she was embarrassed. She was afraid I might tell my son, Jim, who had recently graduated from the Police Academy and become an HPD officer. When I saw the extensive damage to the car, and found out about the accident, (she said it was "only a little scrape, hardly noticeable") I asked her, "Mother, did you stop?"

She answered, "With all those diamonds on my hands? No, I was afraid I would get mugged." Jim never knew Grandma was a fugitive on the run.

Mother's accident (little scrape) took place not long after her friend, Ms. Debbs, made a wrong turn at the airport and somehow ended up on the tarmac, barely missing an airplane. That little incident made the six o'clock news, the ten o'clock news, and the *Houston Chronicle*.

After all those near misses, it wasn't as hard for her to give up the keys, but it was hard for Evelyn, J. L., and me, because then we had lots more to do for Mother—cats to vets, weekly rent to be collected, bills to pay and mail, countless errands to run, groceries to buy, and did I mention she read the newspaper ads to find out where we should go to get the best deals on cat food and litter? Never mind if it was more than ten miles away.

Mother ruled the roost from her recliner in the corner of her bedroom. By the time she was in her late nineties, she reluctantly relented and allowed us to ask some of her renters to clean her house. However, they could only clean as well as she would allow them to. She continued to shout out orders from her throne: "Don't throw that away" or "Don't move this."

The caretakers would only work in four-hour shifts. They couldn't take more than four hours at a time. Mother would not allow anyone to stay with her at night. She said, "I'm not paying someone to sit here and watch me sleep."

The evening worker helped her to bed at about seven o'clock, before she left for the day. If the person on duty was not there by seven o'clock the next morning, she would really squawk and be in a foul mood all day. Needless to say, all of them were usually pretty prompt. They didn't want to work on weekends, so the family took turns visiting and picking up or preparing meals for her. The family was Mother's Meals on Wheels. Mother finally decided she might need someone to spend *some* nights with her.

One Sunday, Evelyn and I arrived at about the same time. We were surprised to find Mother not feeling well and a little incoherent. We decided to call an ambulance. The paramedics told us she was dehydrated and should go to the hospital. Mother told them, "I have cats to take care of. I can't go to the hospital." I reassured her that we would feed the cats and not to worry about them. She was transported to the nearest hospital. Evelyn and I followed her there and stayed with her until late evening when she felt much better. Her Sunday night person came to the hospital to stay.

The next morning, I got ready to go to work. I was still working for the law firm. It was practically next door to the hospital. Just as I was about to turn into my office parking lot, I had the strong feeling that I needed to go by and check on Mother first. I'd planned to go on my lunch break, but something was telling me to get there immediately. When I arrived, her caretaker told me they talked during the night, and she had done well, adding, "She seemed to be much better. However, she stopped talking early this morning."

The doctor and nurses suddenly bombarded me and began to say I only had a few minutes to let them know whether or not to resuscitate. They said I needed to get a signed document to them immediately. I called Judy at the firm where we both worked. She was heading to the hospital with it. About that time, my sister and her husband arrived, just as the doctor was giving Mother an injection to make her heart restart. I told them not to resuscitate by pounding her chest. The injection did not work. They tried again, and within a few minutes, my mother was gone. There had been so much panic and chaos just seconds before, and now, complete and utter silence. I walked over and gently touched her face. At that moment, I felt the strong presence of my grandmother. I think she came to escort her child home. She had waited a long time. Mother was ninety-seven years old when she died on April 29, 2002.

Shortly after Mother's passing, I was in search of comfort and desperately needed the healing process to begin. I found some help in a book. The book was written by hospice care nurses. They are "earth angels" who care for patients toward the end of their lives. The book gave a written account of several terminally ill and aging people. The nurses recorded what the patients saw or said in their final hours. Almost all of them agreed: "Most of the time, the patient sees their own mother as the person (or spirit) that comes to escort them, their loved one, home."

Further, it addresses the age-old question about whether there is a place for our pets in heaven. I read one story about a man who was very attached to his pet bird. His wife was at the hospital with him when he passed away. After his passing, she returned home and found the little bird dead in its cage. Although that was sad, it comforted her because she felt the man's pet had joined him in his passage to heaven. Her belief resonated with my own, which was reinforced by what I personally witnessed after my mother's death.

The morning after Mama died, I went to her house to feed the cats. There, in the driveway at her back yard, lay Felix and Doty or Toby (one of the twins), Mother's two favorite cats—the ones she kept asking me to take home, the ones usually found sitting in her lap. Of all the cats, those two were dead. At the time, it made me really sad. I wished I could have taken them home and protected them. I felt a lot of guilt. I phoned Linda, one of Mother's caretakers, and asked her to have someone come get the two cats and bury them. Later, after reading the book, I felt a great sense of relief. I was thankful I had not lied to appease Mother. It was impossible for me to take them, and I told her so. I truly believe she took them home with her.

I vividly recalled the last time she asked me to adopt them. It was a few weeks before her death. I stopped to visit on my way home from work. Mother had no idea I was no longer living in my house. I had moved to an apartment in Atascocita. I never wanted to tell her. I knew it would bring on a multitude of questions that couldn't be easily answered. By the time I moved to the apartment, one of my own two cats had died. The complex wouldn't allow more than one pet. I didn't feel it was right to continue to blame Bud, and I consoled myself since I had answered truthfully when I said I was not allowed to take her two.

The night before the day of that visit, I made the difficult decision to ask Mother a serious question about my adoption. Although there was no verbal demand "in place," it was a forbidden subject. All of us knew and accepted it as taboo, one we never discussed. I stressed over it most of the night. By morning, I finally worked it out in my mind—how to approach the unapproachable with the unmentionable. That day, I sat in the chair directly in front of her. Nervously, I procrastinated, making small talk. I swallowed the lump that had formed in my throat. My previous plan of approach had fallen by the wayside. In her presence, I couldn't even remember what it was. I tried desperately to rebuild my courage. Finally, I asked, "Mother, was I ever legally adopted?"

She answered me with her own question (a tactic I had learned from the lawyer's years earlier). "Does that bother you?"

After all the years, I still didn't want *her* to think it was something of great importance to me. I was afraid that might hurt her. I answered, "No, I guess not, not really."

I felt a burning sensation in my chest. Tears began to well up inside of me. I wanted to hide my feelings—the ones I was never supposed to have. I struggled to hide them. I fought back the tears and tried to hide any sign of anxiety. Just then, she responded, "Well, I see the tears in your eyes, so I think it must."

I waited ... but that was it! End of conversation. Only seconds before, I had felt totally vulnerable, exposed, near prostrate in front of my own mother ... and for what? I wondered if the lack of an answer *was* the answer. What was the answer?

Mother told us she didn't want to have a funeral because she had outlived all her family and friends. She only wanted a graveside memorial service. She said, "There would be no one left to come."

Mother would have been proud. It was a beautiful service, and many people attended. All her caretakers came, and most of my dear friends were there. I am so blessed to have such wonderful, caring friends, including all three of the attorneys from my office: Frank Gray, Kenneth Burch, and Carl Haddad. The pastor of my church, Brother Harry McDaniel, officiated, and Judy's daughter, Kayla, sang. It was all so beautiful and unforgettable.

I had a difficult time dealing with Mother's passing. When a person is such an all-consuming part of your life, and suddenly he or she is gone, that leaves such a void, not necessarily in a good or a bad way. Inside, a part of me screamed, "What do I do now?" Another part of me was shouting, "Free at last!"

I felt like that little girl again, spinning around on roller skates, with her long hair blowing freely in the wind. The mixed feelings reminded me of stories I read about slaves being set free yet complacently deciding to stay on the plantation. I think *that* reality frightened me into the realization: "I need to find out more about who I am so I can move forward." And I certainly wanted to move forward.

CHAPTER 22

Marriage(s)

Above all else, guard your heart, for it is the wellspring of life.
— Prv 4:23

I've heard it said that we are all products of the choices we make, whether good, bad, or ugly. I'm not exactly sure what influenced my decision-making process early in 2002. I think it was a combination of several things. I had attended funerals of friends who seemed to have barely begun to live when suddenly they were gone. Some of them had been caretakers most of their lives. It frightened me to think that their purpose had been to take care of someone else, and that was all life on this earth had to offer. You live, and then you die. I wanted more—a whole lot more of life and living in between the two. Maybe it was a fear of missing out that caused me to leave my home, move to an apartment, and divorce my husband of thirty-five years.

Throughout the decades, Bud and I had our problems, but we never argued much. We both worked very hard and concentrated on providing a nice home, not an extravagant one, for our family. Neither of us made a lot of money. We realized that if we were to have anything extra, we would have to make more than a paycheck. That is why—a few years earlier—we began to invest in property. It worked for my mother, and there was no reason why it couldn't work for us. We bought one house; made repairs, painted, replaced flooring, and gave it an overall face-lift. We sold it within thirty days of purchase, on the same day as the For Sale sign was placed in the yard. We found our niche. A couple of Realtors asked us to work with them.

After that, we bought rental properties. We worked hard and never took a weekend off. Everybody else was going to the beach, relaxing, or having a good time, but we worked and worked. I came to realize that *work* seemed to be all we did. And we did that really well. I began to wonder if we had anything else in common. I was afraid that we were losing our ability to have *fun* together. Bud's motto was "Work while we can, and there will always be time for fun, later."

Later never did come around. I preferred to work a day and take two off. (I always was a procrastinator.) After a while, I realized that his idea and my idea of *fun* weren't nearly the same. I wanted to go places and see things. He said he had done all that in the navy. It seemed as if we were becoming better friends and work partners than anything else. After all, we *had* grown up together.

The last ten years had actually been pretty smooth sailing. I called them the best years of our marriage. Either we had unwittingly reached some common ground and learned to accept each other, warts and all, or we stayed so busy (working) we didn't notice that we were beginning to drift apart.

We had our problems, the way most couples do. I'll admit that during our first twenty-five years together our ship almost sank a couple of times. But those times, we managed to unload some old baggage, and we kept "the Love Boat" afloat. Those old bags would disappear for a long time. Then, here they would come again—haunting us—bobbing up to the top like Styrofoam coolers filled with unresolved issues.

After a mere twenty-five years, we *both* realized and agreed that unresolved issues could destroy one's health and marriage. Bud began to change his priorities, and so did I. He quit drinking, and his temperament substantially improved. Both of those actions had a positive effect on our relationship.

However, by then we had long since become empty nesters. I was more than ready to fly. He wasn't. We didn't.

It was at that time when I began to think of words like "too late" and "there's too much water under that bridge."

After my mother passed away the same year, my sense of stability was really shaken. Everything around me was changing. I began to question my decisions. Was there any value or practicality in being independent? Although apprehensive about the choices I had made, I continued to look forward in anticipation of my unknown future.

Had I known then what I know now, I might have stayed in my comfort zone. But there *was* that Reba song "Is There Life Out There?" And there *was* my overzealous imagination of what life and love was supposed to look like. Unfortunately, that unrealistic image was fabricated as a result of Disney books and movies—princes and princesses, just one big conglomeration of fairy tales ("… and they lived happily ever after"). I should have paid more attention to endings of films such as *Old Yeller*.

On February 13, 2004, I met my "Oliver." He had beautiful laughing blue eyes. We talked incessantly over never-ending cups of coffee. I left the restaurant and returned to my apartment at four in the morning. My telephone was ringing when I arrived, and I rushed to answer. It was *him*. He wanted to make sure I made it home safely. He asked, "Do you do this to everyone you meet?"

"What?"

"Make them feel this way?"

"Oh, that? Yes."

There was an obvious mutual attraction, and this first encounter led to hours, days, and evenings together. I hadn't danced in years. We danced. There's just something about music and dancing that draws the heart and soul of two people together.

Only a week or so after we met, he called me at work. When I picked up the phone, he asked, "Would you like to go to lunch with me in Paris?" He paused then said, "I wrote your name down as my companion on my fly-form."

He explained that as a pilot he could choose someone to accompany him on flights. I was overwhelmed, so I didn't respond immediately. My mind said this was happening way too fast. I wondered, "Who is this person? Can I trust him?"

Nevertheless, I answered, "Okay."

I could tell that he sensed my reluctance. He said, "I guess this is pretty fast."

It's no wonder our entire relationship moved like a whirlwind. After we hung up, I thought to myself, *what woman wouldn't be swept off her feet? Isn't this the answer to my dreams of wanting to go places and see things?*

Against my better judgment, I convinced myself this was real, and *he* was real. I *knew* in my heart it was all too good to be true. I allowed myself to believe I had found my prince, my knight, and my magical Disney movie began to unfold before my very eyes. Lucky me! I was cast in the leading role as princess.

We were married on September 18, 2004, and the princess, true to her dreams, *did* get to go many places and see many things. If the marriage itself could be described in one word, it would be *tragicomedy*. My magical Disney movie turned into one more version of *The War of the Roses* (without the chandelier).

We made it through several years of marriage, but in the end and in the best interest of both of us, we had to reach an agreement to disagree. Eventually that became something we could both successfully agree on.

We divorced in December 2010.

Bud and I have shared a home since 2011. We are "housemates." We don't always agree on everything (we realize we don't have to), but we do have mutual respect for each other. Neither of us holds a grudge; we are both secure in how the other one feels, and, more importantly, we are able to forgive one another. Each Sunday morning (when our health allows) he gets up, gets ready, and heads off to his church. I get ready and go to mine. We know that we have so much to be thankful for. The two of us shared thirty-five years of good times and hard times. We kissed one another goodbye every morning, as we both headed off to work each day, even when one or the other didn't feel like going. There's so much to be said about having a shared history. The good memories are precious, especially when it comes to grandchildren. Besides, who else would understand when I asked, "Remember when Mother …?"

The two of us have a unique relationship. Not only do we have a long past history in common, but we are there to help each other. We have also learned to listen to one another. Contrary to popular opinion, there is a lot to be said for being predictable and consistent. Lord, how I wanted, needed, and have grown to appreciate, consistency in my life.

I don't believe that any years of my life have been wasted. I won't allow myself to think that. I have come to believe that time and experience mixed together served as fertilizer to stretch and grow me. And I can't help but think that throughout my life, I have gone through an awful lot of stretching and growing for a special purpose. Perhaps it was to prepare *me*, to help someone else get through some difficult situation. My belief, faith, and hours spent in Christian counseling continue to serve me well every day.

CHAPTER 23

Gloria

"Vickie," the pastor said again. "I believe you have a few words to share with us."

I gathered my notes and book, *More Stories for the Heart*. I got out of my chair and stepped up to the podium, took a deep breath, and began by telling the attendees about my discovery of a beautiful poem, appropriate for such an occasion as this, adding that I would like to share some of it. I told them I knew nothing about the "unknown" author but felt we had a lot in common.

I explained that a couple of weeks earlier, when first seeing the poem "Legacy of an Adopted Child," I was immediately drawn to the title. After reading it, I became filled with emotion. I found it in my book *More Stories for the Heart. Thinking how rare it was to find such a unique work*, I knew it must be shared with the group, "Today, I am reassured of God's perfect timing. I know that when something like this happens, it is a gift from God—something special and meant to be. Finding the perfect words at the right time is further proof of His hand in action. Before He gave me this gift in the form of a book, I had no idea what I might say that could convey my message in such an unusual set of circumstances. I'll never forget how I could almost hear the voices of both moms' reciting the words with me as I read.

Legacy of an Adopted Child
— Author Unknown

Once there were two women, who never knew each other,

One you may not remember, the other you call Mother.

I stood in front of friends and family, distracted for a moment by the words, which continued to flow through my mind. It was all I could do to keep my tears from following suit and flowing down my cheeks. My voice cracked a little as I came to my favorite two lines.

One gave you emotions; the other calmed your fears,

One saw your first sweet smile, the other dried your tears.

I explained that the poem continued on with the same type of beautifully written lyrics and attributes, ending with the age-old question and topic of debate. Is it heredity or environment that gives a child his or her traits? In this case, the poet states, "It is neither: just two different kinds of love."

Afterward I talked about how Gloria and I had developed a unique relationship over the years, becoming the best of friends. "I visited her a few times, but we talked regularly on the telephone. The phone conversations allowed us to get to know one another. She had become a good Christian woman, and through hardship and sickness, she had come to rely on her faith. Gloria had several bouts with cancer, and until now she had been able to overcome the disease. This time, it caught her off guard. She was so weak that her frail body could not fight another battle."

I told the small group I was reminded of the short story "Calm in the Storm." It is about a woman of great faith, caught in a frightening storm in the middle of the Atlantic Ocean. She kept all the little children on board from panicking by telling Bible stories.

Afterward, when the ship safely docked, the captain asked the lady how she had remained calm during the rough storm when everyone else was afraid the ship might sink.

She responded that she had two daughters. She said, "One of them lives in New York. The other lives in heaven. I knew I would see one or the other of my daughters in a few hours. And it really didn't matter to me which one."

Her faith had not allowed her to worry; it brought her great peace.

I made a comparison between that brave woman and Gloria. "The raging storm had come in the disguise of cancer, which by then had consumed her body. Gloria knew her son, Harold, was on his way, due to arrive soon. But if she failed to make it through her own storm, she would be in heaven with her other son, Jim. Knowing she would soon be with one of her two sons had to offer great comfort and peace in her final hours. I am so thankful for God's grace."

Although I had volunteered to speak at her funeral, (feeling it was the last good thing I could do for my birth mother) I was anxious to return to my chair and resume the train of thought I had been on before my name was called. The mental trip had begun days before, upon first receiving the call from Harold, notifying me of her death. Random thoughts and unanswered questions raced through my mind. I realized that when Gloria and I talked, we only spoke of current things. Call it naive, but neither one of us wanted to dredge up the past or the five W's: who, what, when, where, and why. Instead, we chose to accept each day and each conversation as a blessing, then move forward with forgiveness and not dwell on past mistakes. Still, there were many things left unsaid, questions left unanswered, and stories left untold. Procrastination was our friend. It had been our way of protecting ourselves from further pain. Or at the very least, a way of delaying it. Now it was past the time to try and make sense of the haphazard course my strange life always seemed to follow.

We exited the funeral home and got into our waiting cars, in-line and prepared for the trip to Martin, Tennessee. Gloria would be laid to rest next to my brother, Jim. The trip from Memphis would be a long one and the near-freezing January rain, traffic and icy wet roads would slow us down.

When we finally arrived at the cemetery, it was still sprinkling cold rain. The grave site was on an incline. I used my umbrella as a cane to steady my balance and keep me from sliding down into the mud.

It had been twenty-one years since I had been there to visit Jim's grave. I remembered that trip well but didn't remember the surroundings. In my memory, Jim's grave was shaded by big, beautiful trees. I had placed a wreath on his headstone, and it seemed to me that his final resting place was peaceful and secluded. Of course, the trees would be asleep now, even if they had still been there. But they weren't. They were gone. Always before, the very thought of them had been such a comfort to me. They represented shade in summer's sweltering heat. They offered a place to kneel down and pray or rest on a cool white bench.

What was I thinking? The trees and seclusion must have given way to so many people and families over the years. The cemetery had become just as congested as the wet roads we traveled to get there. I closed my eyes and forced my mind to switch gears. While the fragrance of dank open earth hovered all around, I began to focus on the joy of a loving reunion between a mother and her son after forty years. I was certain it had been Jim who came to escort his mother home.

JUDY and VICKIE

On the way back to Memphis, we stopped to eat. The restaurant reminded me of one we had gone to in 1986, when Judy and I visited. That time, several of Dale's family members took all of us to eat. We were seated and given menus. When the waitress asked Gloria for her order, she responded, "I think I will have this roast beef with au jus gravy, Aujus, Awjuice." Judy blurted out, "Gesundheit!" The whole table laughed, including Gloria. She had been trying so hard to properly pronounce the gravy. She loved attention but certainly didn't want to draw any negative attention. Still, she couldn't help but laugh, and I loved that she could laugh at herself. Here we were, twenty-one years later. I was thinking about how much she would have enjoyed this gathering. Gloria's absence was ever-present, just as it is today.

Three years later, Dale passed away. He died in 2010 on (what would have been) Gloria's birthday, March 2 Coincidently, that happened to be the day Bud and I got married, forty-three years earlier, March 2, 1967. Back then, I hadn't known it was her birthday. Even more strange, our son, Jim, and his wife, Stefanie, married on Bud's mother's birthday, April 8, without realizing it. Sometimes I feel obsessed with correlating numbers, dates and events. Must be the bookkeeper in me. It has never helped when picking lotto numbers.

About a year after Dale's death, I felt it was important to tell Harold what I had been told years earlier (when I was only ten) concerning the possibility of having another brother. We discussed it a few times; both unaware of any truth there may, or may not be, to the rumor. We felt neither Dale nor his family would have known anything about it, since he came into Gloria's life some years later. Neither one of us wanted to share the information with others or ask questions that might encourage more rumors or questions.

Harold said, "Growing up, Mom never mentioned anything about having another child."

We made the decision to keep Gloria's "best kept secret" to ourselves, *if* there really was one. Neither Harold nor I wanted to be guilty of creating undue suspicion or hint at an unconfirmed rumor by discussing it with others. We figured if it was true, there would not be many people left from back then to say so, and I have learned that country folks *can* keep a secret.

Over the next few years when Harold and I talked on the phone, the idea of having another brother was never too far from our thoughts. One of us came up with the idea of having a DNA test. Since there was the possibility of another sibling, he and I wondered if we had the same birth father.

CHAPTER 24

Rodney/Kenneth

Can a mother forget the baby at her breast and have no compassion
on the child she has borne? Though she may forget, I will not
forget you! See, I have engraved you on the palms of my hands.
— Is 49:15–16

On May 7, 2013, Harold and I each received shocking yet amazing
phone calls. Both were from a lady who worked for Tennessee
Children's Services. She placed a call to each of us. She informed
both of us that we had a sibling who was trying to make contact.
She verified some information and asked if we would be interested
in allowing our brother to get in touch. We both eagerly said yes.
Protocol was that she had to send paperwork to be filled out. We
both received the forms to be completed and hurriedly returned them
to her at the department. She called to acknowledge receipt of the
returned papers on May 22, 2013. That is when time began to drag.

About six months went by, and we heard nothing from our
brother. Harold and I were calling one another almost daily to
compare information, or lack thereof. We had no idea where our
brother was. We didn't even know his name. The department could
not give us any information about him since he had been the one
who initiated the search.

Finally, I called the representative back to tell her we had received
no response from our brother. I confirmed that she had everything
needed to get the ball rolling. I didn't expect she would be able to
do anything about it. However, this considerate lady kindly offered
to call him. She would ask if he had changed his mind about the
contact. I held my breath, fearing he was having second thoughts. She
called him the next day and then called us back. She said he had been
ill but would call soon. It was a great relief to know he still planned

on calling. However, it was disconcerting to discover he had been ill. Again, the wait was agonizing. Was it something serious? Could his illness be terminal? Considering Gloria's medical history, our minds were susceptible to various negative interpretations, which led to lots of worry and concern on our parts.

It was not until the end of December 2014—one year and seven months after the initial phone call informing us of his existence—when I heard my brother's voice for the first time in my life. I had almost given up hope. I was at work the day he called. He left a phone message on my home answering machine. The voice on the recorder said, "Vickie, this is your brother, Rodney, uh, born, Kenneth Eugene Barnes. I will call you again."

I played the message two or three times, savoring the very sound of his voice. I looked at the caller ID, got the number, and impatiently called it back. We talked over an hour that night. Many times I had wondered what our first conversation might be like. When I thought about it, I would become apprehensive and nervous, but as soon as Rodney said, "Hello," we talked as though we had known one another for the last sixty-three years. We had lots of catching up to do.

I discovered that Rodney's birthday is in May, only one day before Bud's. I asked what his favorite cake is. His answer absolutely, positively, confirmed our brother-sister relationship: "german chocolate." He told me he wanted to call on Christmas Day. He gave reasons why he hadn't: He was too nervous about doing it. He didn't want to bother us during our family Christmas gathering. He didn't know what we might have to talk about. I reassured him, stating, "We have an entire lifetime to share."

The truth is, there was far more talking to be done then we could possibly have time left on this earth. I didn't want to lose one more minute of it. The reason he had not called sooner was because he had been recuperating from cancer but had recently been given a clean bill of health. God is good.

Rodney told me he had been placed in an orphanage in Selmer, Tennessee, and two wonderful people had adopted him when he was just six months old. He said he had a good life with very kind parents and added, "But I always felt like I had a sister."

He told me that when his mother (our mother) had delivered him to the orphanage, she placed a little toy lamb in his crib. Apparently, the new parents took the lamb with them. He always kept it. He lived in many homes and moved several times during his life because his father was a United Methodist minister. Both his parents were now deceased, and his brother, David, had passed away a few years back. At that time, my standard last sentence (before we hung up) was "I don't know you, but I love you."

Harold; his wife, Carol; Bud; and I made plans to meet Rodney for the first time, in Mississippi, in June 2015. That was only six months away. The anticipation was overwhelming.

CHAPTER 25

Truth

Before I formed you in the womb I knew you.
— Jer 1:5

In the summer, June 2014, which was a year after Harold and I discovered we had a brother, and a year before we actually met him, Bud and I made a trip to Ohio to visit Bud's brother, Philip; his wife, Sylvia; daughter, Karen; and other family members. On our way, we stopped in Corinth, Mississippi, and stayed a couple of nights with my aunt Doris and her son, Johnny. I was so happy to see them. It had been many years. After the others went to sleep, Aunt Doris and I caught up on sixty-plus years of stories. I feel so blessed that Aunt Doris (at the age of ninety) is still with us and has such a good memory.

In that late-night marathon conversation, we discussed everything and everyone we could remember. I asked her if she remembered Unckie.

"Do you mean Uncle Herb? He was your daddy's brother, wasn't he?"

"All of us kids gave him the nickname Unckie, but he was no relation to anyone in the family. Mother told me he had been in the navy, served at Pearl Harbor, and afterward, came to Houston looking for work. Daddy gave him a job at his store. Daddy couldn't pay enough for him to live on, so eventually he rented a room in their house. That is how he came to live with them."

"One time, Grady was gone and Uncle Herb came next door to my house. He made me feel uncomfortable," Aunt Doris said.

"What happened?" I asked.

"He said, 'If you ever leave Grady, I want you.'"

"What do you mean?" I asked.

"He told me, 'I want you for mine. I want you for my own.'"

I was surprised at my uncle's audacity, but I tried not to show it. I wondered if that was one of those times when he sneaked out and had a few too many to drink.

"Daddy's sisters always thought he and Mother had a thing." I smiled when I told her and then continued on with my story.

"Once, when we were in the eleventh grade, my friend Carol and I went to Corpus Christi to visit Aunt Alene and Aunt Christine. They passed away years ago, but back then, both asked me about the relationship between Unckie and Mother. I thought the question was odd and sort of funny. I assured them there was nothing going on because we kids would have known. I was taken aback at the very idea."

"Everyone knew they were having an affair," Aunt Doris said. Her casual tone and response shocked me. She was just as composed with this revelation as I was startled by it. Calmly, she continued.

"One time, I had to take Johnny to the doctor, and I asked Alma to babysit you. When I came back to get you, I asked Grandma where Alma was. Grandma pointed upstairs with a frown on her face. I started to leave, and Grandma said, "You don't have to leave. Go on up and get her.""

Aunt Doris said she got upstairs and could hear talking. She heard Alma tell Herb, "This is *our* baby."

Aunt Doris said she pushed on the partially open door, and I was there in the bed, between the two of them. She said, "Alma was in her nightgown lying on the bed."

I told my aunt, "This is a flashback from my early childhood—laughing and playing hide-n-seek under the covers—but in my memory, the two grownups were Melzar and whoever he was seeing at the time."

Then I thought back on the terrible accusations Mother had made about me to Bud, about Evelyn, and about Billy's wife. When I even tried to imagine it, her story seemed so far-fetched; it didn't make any sense. I couldn't understand how anyone (even Mother) could be that hypocritical, so I decided to "test" Aunt Doris.

"When you went upstairs, did you turn right or left to get to that room?" I asked her.

"I turned right at the top of the stairs."

I had never known my aunt Doris to lie, and evidently she was telling the truth now. I'm not sure why—maybe because I had heard, "If you verbalize something painful, it becomes easier to cope with"—but I felt compelled to share my tragic and only once before disclosed secret with her.

I told her, "A few years ago, I went to a Christian counselor to get to the root of some serious problems I was dealing with. I had never before said the words out loud, but, through uncontrollable tears, I managed to tell her that my uncle had molested me during those early years, between the ages of three and five, when I first went to live there. It was buried in a dark place, deep within my mind, but I always knew it happened, and I always felt guilty about it."

My counselor seemed shocked when she asked me, "And you've never told anyone about this before?"

I answered, "No, never."

She said, "Victims always blame themselves."

I told my aunt, "I think what she said is true about victims blaming themselves. Unckie had been in the navy, and he had nightmares about Pearl Harbor. He hollered out in his sleep. His screams woke me up, and I was so terrified that I would get out of my bed, cross the small hallway at the top of the stairs, and go into his room. When Billy came to live with us (his room was next door to mine), Unckie's nightmares seemed to subside. After that, I began to have nightmares of my own. I still remember waking up frightened many nights and walking downstairs to crawl into bed with Mother. I had a recurring dream of hundreds of snakes piled on top of one another, and they covered the ground where I tried to walk."

I think the story must have left Aunt Doris speechless. How do you respond to something like that? I never spoke the words out loud again. My healing will have to come from the written word.

I told Aunt Doris, "The State of Tennessee Children's Services contacted Harold and me, to tell us we have another sibling, but we have not yet heard from him. Since we discovered there was another brother, we wondered about our own relationship to one another. We talked about it several times before Harold and I decided to have a DNA test. We discovered that we are more than likely half-siblings." I added, "That begs an answer to the question, do you know who my real father might be?"

Aunt Doris said, "I always wondered what happened to little Kenneth. I saw him after he was born. He was a beautiful baby."

I was surprised to find out that she knew my newly revealed brother's birth name, and she had actually seen him. Country folks sure can keep a secret.

All my recently discovered information, which I had been ready and willing to share with Aunt Doris, came as no surprise to her. Although seemingly quiet about many things, she did offer up a "likely-hood" story about a fellow (a felon) by the name of Russ Hamilton.

Like every other McNairy County resident, Aunt Doris has her copy of *Walking Tall*. When that book became a hit movie in the 1970s, Bufford Pusser, who was elected sheriff of the county, became a household name. Pusser served as sheriff from 1964 until 1970. He waged war on moonshining, gambling, prostitution, the State Line Mob, and the Dixie Mafia. He became a local hero and survived multiple stabbings and shootings. The sheriff was forced to kill several people during his career, and one such person was Charles Russell Hamilton. Russ Hamilton had reportedly killed a deputy named York in Chewalla, Tennessee, (where I was born) back when Bufford Pusser was just a small child. Through the years, Hamilton killed more people, including his wife, who he beat to death. Furthermore, he supposedly had something to do with the death of his own mother. Apparently, he was the town's true-to-life "bad guy."

On Christmas Day 1968, the Sheriff's Department received a frantic phone call from Hamilton's landlord, stating that he (Hamilton) was drunk and was threatening to kill him and his wife. Sheriff Pusser responded to the call. When he arrived, Hamilton was cordial and invited him in. I guess when the sheriff went to arrest him; things became a lot less friendly. The details of the shootout are blurry, but Hamilton's gun was fired multiple times. One shot grazed the sheriff and another shattered the grip of his revolver. The sheriff then drew his .357 Magnum Colt, fired one shot, and hit Hamilton between the eyes, killing him before he hit the floor. Sheriff Pusser said, "I was forced to kill the man." He was exonerated by a McNairy County grand jury.

I was born on October 19, 1948, in a little house next door to a relative of Russ Hamilton. Aunt Doris said he spent lots of time at his relative's house. She said it wasn't unusual to see him make the trek next door several times a day. She thought it was strange and questionable why the man insisted on being present at my birth. She told me, "It wouldn't be too far a stretch of the imagination if he might be your father." She added, "I hated to even say it, and I probably shouldn't have told you."

I guess she was able to read my mixed expressions of doubt, disbelief, and disappointment, because she quickly added, "Russ was not a bad man when he wasn't drinking. He used to walk by our house. If we were outside, he always had a smile and said hello. I wasn't afraid of him like some people were. He was always courteous and nice to me. He was a good-looking man. He was an Indian and had that kind of dark complexion. I don't think he was really *bad*, he just couldn't drink."

Dazed and confused, I wondered if my adopted mother had known any of those little details. If she had even *thought* this guy might be my birth father, it would explain why early on, when I was too little to understand what she was talking about, she began to tell me how I had alcohol in my "genes." *Alcohol! Nothing! My genes could be riddled with serial killer.*

I suppose all those words about Russ not being a "bad" guy were meant to make me feel better. I guess I must have just been coming out of a stupor, or I was trying to process what was being said, because I couldn't respond, except to stare at Aunt Doris. Again, she quickly added, "But I always thought you were Melzar's."

Well, so did I. Suddenly, Melzar didn't sound so bad—child profiteer vs. murderer—do the math. Throughout the years when I met members of the Barnes family and saw pictures of them, I always felt there was a close resemblance. But, there *was* that DNA, and DNA doesn't lie. Just watch your courtroom drama on television. The markers were very, very close on our tests, but the report said Harold and I are "more than likely half-siblings." Maybe we should call for a redo.

To say that Aunt Doris's suggestion did not pique my interest would be a false statement. Perhaps it was not *interest* nearly so much as it was a need to prove her possible theory wrong. I decided, then and there, that as soon as I spoke with Virginia again, I would pursue an answer.

Virginia is the older sister of twins, Lurline and Geraldine, all daughters of Archie and Vinnie. Gloria and Virginia were raised together and were more like sisters than cousins. *If anyone would know anything, surely it would be her.*

I asked Virginia if she had ever heard that Jim and Harold might have a different father than I. After a long, pregnant pause, Virginia said, "I did hear something like that."

I know how close she and Gloria were, and I knew it would not be something she could easily talk about. Still, I pressed the issue. Since mine and Harold's DNA test numbers were so close, I asked, "Did you ever hear it could have been a family member?"

She said, "No, but I had already moved to Memphis at that time. I didn't know much about what was going on back home." She added, "I will ask the twins if they ever heard anything like that."

The next time we talked, she said, "There was the rumor you had a different father, but once you were born, you looked so much like a Barnes, the rumor died."

That did answer one of my questions. Did it also answer the other? If anything, it left me even more confused and curious. Virginia added, "If Gloria didn't want to talk about something, no one could get her to say a word. She never liked to talk about her life from back then."

After all the information I had collected, I could clearly understand why. But I was tired of all the secrets. If anyone knew anything, I wanted to know. It seemed to me that people were trying to protect my feelings. They didn't lie to me *if* I "asked the right questions," but weren't they lying by omission, if they did know something and kept it to themselves? I had to drag information out of them. The whole thing was beginning to feel more like a cover-up.

More than likely, there are people who would say, "After all these years, what difference does it make who your father is?" Maybe it doesn't. It simply comes down to my right to know.

On that night of "truth," Aunt Doris told me that when Mother made them move, essentially abandoning me those years ago, they rented a house on Lila Lane, less than a mile from where they left me. They stayed in the same area until I graduated from high school. She said she was at my baptism and my graduation. She kept up with me through neighbors and friends. Occasionally, she saw a picture of me in the local newspaper, the *Sentinel*.

I asked her if she had known the Bookouts. She said, "Yes, they were my neighbors." I told her I remembered going to a party in junior high at Richard Bookout's house on Lila Lane. She knew, because she had seen me there. Although I was an adult with grandchildren when I found all that out, I don't think I had ever felt such a sense of rejection or abandonment as I did at that moment. I told her how much I had needed her during those years, just to talk with. Aunt Doris said she understood, but she had made a promise to my mother and felt obligated to fulfill it.

After that conversation, and after I returned home from our visit, Aunt Doris wrote a letter to tell me how sorry she was. She didn't realize that telling me she lived there for so long, without my knowing, would hurt me so badly. How could she not have known? Didn't she know how much she meant to me, how long I waited and prayed that someday she would return for me? I don't know why she told me. Maybe she was looking for absolution. She didn't need to. After I got past the initial hurt and pain, I remembered the most important thing: Aunt Doris was there for me during my formative years when I had no one else. At a time when she had a choice, she chose to treat me as if I was her own. She even called me her own when she said, "Now I have my little boy and my little girl." I can't remember another time in my childhood when I felt that kind of unconditional love. She will always be the "angel" I saw in her, with eyes of a loving and trusting child.

Doris Barnes passed away on March 12, 2019 just before book was finished. To My Aunt Doris: Anyone who knew her had to have known that she couldn't linger long without "her Johnny." Thank you for sharing secrets with me and for saying, "I love the book." Hearing you laugh made the challenges of writing it twice as meaningful. I wish we could have finished reading it together and as you said, "had time to make more of the good memories." But you were called and you never cared for putting off until tomorrow what needed to be done today. I will forever love you and miss you.

CHAPTER 26

Reunion

L-R, Harold, Virginia, Me, Rodney, Standing in below pic is Bud

Bud and I left Texas early and arrived in Batesville, Mississippi, before dark on Saturday, June 7, 2015. We were to pick up my newfound brother on Sunday morning, June 8. After that, we would head to Memphis, Tennessee, where Rodney would meet our brother, Harold, and his wife, Carol. They had flown in from Detroit, Michigan, for this very special occasion. It had been eight years since Gloria's funeral. That was when Harold, Carol, and I had last seen one another. Harold and I were going to meet Rodney, our brother, for the first time in our lives.

After my sleepless night, with all the excitement and anticipation of a child on the night before Christmas, Bud and I left the hotel that morning and drove toward Rodney's home. Rodney lived with friends he had gone to school with, Buster and his wife, Nancy. Buster's parents had been close friends with Rodney's adoptive parents, and the two boys had known one another most of their lives. A road sign told us it was less than twenty miles away. Each passing mile left me feeling more anxious. All kinds of things can run through a person's mind: "Will he like me?" "Will I be a disappointment?" "Will we look alike?"

Bud and I followed a beautifully tree-lined winding country road for miles. Occasionally, we saw uprooted and fallen trees left behind from the last big storm that had swept through. There were deer crossing signs along the route, so that forced us to slow down. Meanwhile, the anticipation continued to build. My heartbeat echoed the sound of the truck tires as they hit the pavement.

I knew we were near the house, but I thought we had gone too far. We pulled into the next driveway to turn around. I could see Nancy's face glowing with a radiant smile, as she hurried out to the truck to meet us. She looked exactly like her Facebook picture. Buster followed close behind. I got out of the truck, and Nancy gave me a genuine Mississippi welcoming hug. It was as real and warm as a freshly baked Mississippi Mud Cake straight from the oven. In the near distance, I saw the screen door open and a man standing on the porch. I could see that he had beautiful white hair and a white full beard. He wore a pair of blue denim shorts, tennis shoes and a black T-shirt. I asked her, "Is that Rodney?" She said, "Yes, that's your brother." Her words were so matter of fact about someone I barely knew existed. They confirmed what I had been longing for and waiting on for so long. I had to choke back my tears. He seemed a little reluctant to join us, almost shy, but I raised my right hand and waved. As he walked in my direction, tears filled my eyes, and I noticed his tears as well. I wasn't sure why we cried. Were they tears of joy from the discovery of this old/new relationship, or were they tears of sadness for the lost time that we could never get back? It was probably a little of both. But I didn't want to waste any time crying, and I certainly didn't want to look back. Wouldn't that mean I wanted to live in the past? I knew better than that. I would never want to settle for life without my brother again. God gave the two of us a chance, and I quickly made *my* choice.

Rodney and I embraced one another with open arms. Neither of us wanted to quit hugging first. When we did, the two of us just looked into each other's eyes. I saw so much in those deep, dark eyes—sincerity, tenderness, kindness, sadness, and lots of love. Just then, Buster walked up to join us. Nancy introduced him and said, "Look at their eyes, Buster; they're just alike." It is true. We both have those dark brown eyes. I could only hope that Rodney had seen in mine the reflection of the qualities I saw in his.

We all went into the house and visited for about an hour. That was when I had the opportunity to tell Rodney that I had received the results from our DNA test. They had arrived at my house the day before we left on our trip.

He said, "We *are* full brother and sister, aren't we?" His words were more of a statement than a question.

Sadly, I had to tell him no. The test revealed that he and I are "more than likely half-siblings." It read the exact same way about his and Harold's test: "more than likely half-siblings." All three of us were "half-siblings." Nancy asked, "Who is Rodney's father?"

I told her that I didn't want to share what others told me. As far as I was concerned, anything I heard was a rumor until proven, and nothing had been 100 percent confirmed.

I explained to Nancy, "I'm the only one with very little idea, and certainly no real evidence, of who my birth father is. There is confirmation of an affair, and I have heard about rumors from that time, so I could take a guess. But it would only be a guess because no one will come forward to give me any direct answers. Maybe no one really knows at all, or maybe they don't want to say out loud what is suspected to be true."

Just then, I couldn't help but think of Nathaniel Hawthorne's character, poor "Mrs. Hester Prynne," all dressed up in her scarlet red dress with the hand-stitched letter *A* beautifully embroidered in golden threads across her chest. She stood in front of the masses, held her baby girl tightly against her bosom, and (surely with hand to brow) declared: "And my child must seek a heavenly Father; she shall never know an earthly one!"

Was I to become another baby Prynne? Would it be that I too shall never know an earthly father? (Methinks I doest think too much!)

After that discussion we left. Rodney would soon meet his brother, Harold.

When we got to the hotel, Carol was standing out front with a big smile on her face. She directed us, like a parking attendant who loved her job, to an available parking space. To say this gathering was full of excitement would be an understatement. Harold was waiting for us inside, and it was something *grandiose* to see these two brothers, two grown men, embrace and welcome one another with open arms. We sat in the reception room for a long time and talked while Carol took pictures.

We all went to dinner that night, but I couldn't wait to get back to the hotel so we could talk and begin to get to know our brother. Besides that, we had a big, Texas-size, beautiful and delicious-looking german chocolate cake with four (count 'em, four) layers waiting for us when we returned to our suite. In our first phone conversation, I asked Rodney about his birthday: month, day, and year. It is May 25, 1951. Since Bud's is May 26, and we all *love* a celebration, especially one that involves food, I felt we could all share a belated birthday party for both of them. It was the first and only birthday party the three of us siblings had ever attended together. Let the festivities begin! I brought the cake with us, all the way from Houston. It tasted just as good as it looked. It was truly a grand celebration—one that I wished Gloria could have attended. And maybe she did. Who could know for sure?

After our cake and coffee celebration, we were anxious to get started and find out more about one another. Harold is outgoing— always telling jokes—and he never meets a stranger. He has no trouble engaging in conversation. Rodney is just the opposite. He is soft-spoken and reserved. When he does speak, people tend to listen because they don't want to miss anything.

He told us about his adopted brother, David, who had passed away five years earlier. He said, "After our adoptive parents passed away, David contacted his biological family, but they had no interest in reuniting."

That had a negative impact on Rodney. In fear of rejection, he procrastinated about getting in touch with his own family. Then Rodney told his own tragic story of loss. It may have been the catalyst that encouraged him to locate us. He said, "I sold my parents' house and bought my home in Memphis. My home burned to the ground. The Fire Department said it was caused by an electrical wiring problem. All my family pictures, albums, and my mother's antiques were in the house. My little dog was sixteen years old. He died in the fire. Only a few things were saved. I had nothing to drive because my truck had been parked in the garage. I didn't have insurance of any kind. That was the first time in my life that I had nothing and no ties to anything."

I guess he left with the money in his pocket, the shirt on his back, and a mind-set of "What do I do next?" Clearly, he was in a state of depression when he took off walking toward Louisiana. His adopted father, a United Methodist minister, and the family lived in several different places during their lifetimes.

I asked him, "Why Louisiana? Did you have friends there? Did you think there would be someone who might remember you and your family?"

He responded, "Yes, I guess that might have been one reason."

He added, "Then I walked to Florida."

Smiling, I asked, "Who are you, Gump?"

He laughed and said, "Yeah, I thought of him. I hitchhiked along the way and took day jobs. I couldn't take a permanent job because I was on the move."

His travels took him to a few other states but eventually brought him back to Memphis.

He said, "It was pouring down rain when I stopped to rest on a bench in front of a restaurant. The manager came out and told me I would be more comfortable on the covered patio, behind the place, out of the rain. It was really cold, but someone brought me a blanket, and I slept on a bench."

After that, he went to a shelter. Someone who worked there asked him if he was a vet. Since he is a veteran, that person helped him get in touch with someone else. Before long, he had money and an income. Thank God for the VA!

He rented an apartment in Memphis. I guess he had walked off a lot of his depression, because he was ready to set up housekeeping again. By that time, Rodney had a telephone and an address.

His good friends from school, Buster and Nancy, heard about the fire. They had been looking for him. They called and asked if he would like to come live with them. He said, "I think I would."

He was tired of the city, and the country atmosphere appealed to him. Also, he was tired of being alone. It wasn't too long after that when Rodney began his search for us, his siblings.

Rodney was so open and honest with us. My brother was a *real* person without a pretense in the world.

The story tugged at my heartstrings, and I thought about the many homeless people standing on corners near where I work. We don't know anything about them, their circumstances, or how they got where they are. Like a lot of people, I am unsure and distrustful of most, but I thought of one man in particular. He was thin with a long white beard and dark, piercing eyes. He held up a small, ragged sign with the word *VET* written on it. I gave him some money, and he gave me a "God bless you." I remembered thinking how we each needed what the other had to offer.

Harold and I told Rodney he never had to feel alone again. We said, "You now know that you have a brother and a sister who love you, and we will be there if you need us." We have all chosen to leave off the "half" when we talk about our relationship to one another.

These are not the only things we learned during our visit with Rodney, not at all. Rodney came with lots of papers. He brought all the information he gathered in his search, and he shared it with us. The names and circumstances were pretty foreign to him, but Carol and I took the bundle and quickly deciphered the ones of major importance—the papers that revealed information previously unknown to or unconfirmed by any of us. Ironically, the printed answer as to the identity of his biological father was found there within the paperwork that Rodney had received months earlier from the Tennessee Children's Welfare Department. The answer had been there in plain sight, all along:

Gloria Barnes' story is the case of an early marriage of two young people. The husband entered the service about two months after the January 3, 1946, birth of twin boys. When he was discharged from the Army, there continued to be infrequent visits to the home, then finally separation. Gloria gave birth to a daughter on October 19, 1948. She and Melzar Barnes were divorced on June 22, 1950. Kenneth Eugene Barnes was born May 25, 1951. Since Gloria was divorced, the child was born out of wedlock and the mother was considered sole guardian. The alleged father, whose name is given as Charles Russell Hamilton, is described by people who know him as being a fine looking man. His hair and eyes are dark, almost black. His complexion is olive and his weight, approximately 155 pounds. He has the manner and demeanor of an Indian. When he is sober, he's friendly, nice and sociable. He is not feeble-minded. He has a son about 16 years old who attends high school. Too much is not known about this man as he is incarcerated. The alleged father did not assume any responsibility for Gloria or her child.

Note: A close relative told me that she was certain, "This man forced himself on Gloria, and she was the victim of rape." I couldn't help but wonder about the reason(s) for his incarceration. The information regarding the alleged rape has not been confirmed.

The mother was placed in a foster home on April 2, 1951. Shortly after her arrival, Gloria had a psychological examination. Before testing, she talked freely of her various problems. The psychologist determined, "She is a woman who at present is under considerable stress. She is obviously a dependent individual and relies heavily on the guidance of others. It would seem advisable for all factors to be studied very carefully concerning her releasing her child for adoption. Such a move might be very disturbing to her in the future, particularly since she appears to be very much attached to the three children she now has." Her own father and step-mother refused to keep her during her pregnancy. An uncle agreed to pay her board of $35 per month if she was removed from her home to another community. Her father and relatives are interested in the three older children and are willing to assist in their care but refuse to accept the baby.

The baby is breast-fed and the mother is happy in making plans for reuniting her family. She is with the child constantly. She tells the foster mother (at the home) that she feels her father might allow her to stay at his house until some permanent arrangement can be made for her and her son. When the case worker takes Gloria and the baby to visit her father (who is in the field dusting cotton), the house remains locked, even though Gloria makes her presence known to her father. The case worker then takes Gloria and her baby to the home of Reverend Moore where they are warmly received by the minister, his wife, and children. They stay there for a couple of weeks before returning to the foster home.

On June 13, 1951, Mrs. Barnes receives a court order from her divorced husband giving him custody of the three older children. The court took them from her and placed them with the father when she became illegally pregnant. The case worker is in her car with Gloria, explaining to her what had happened. The twins and their sister had been placed (for about three months) in separate foster homes, in the same community. There, they could share the same church and Sunday school as both foster families were good friends. The children were beginning to be well-adjusted in their foster homes. The twins were no longer afraid of darkness and would enter the house alone. Their eating habits were now normal. Their actions, also, were normal. The little girl was apparently well-adjusted in her foster home. On June 13, 1951, the three children were removed from their foster homes, by court order, to be placed in the custody of their father, Melzar Barnes. This was done with little preparation of the children and was a tearful and traumatic experience. Gloria screams and cries, stating, "He cannot do this to me as I have not received any papers". The case worker urges her to think of her baby and says plans can be worked out later for the other children. She tells Gloria that she is in no condition now to take her complaint to court.

On July 27, 1951, Gloria and her baby return to her father's home. They stay in a small room which is completely filled with furniture.

The room has only one window and it is too hot to sleep. They both become ill and are taken to the doctor where they are treated. Gloria explains to the doctor that it is necessary for her to be separated from her baby in order to obtain employment. She is stimulated by a desire for a job that will enable her to re-unite her family. The doctor gives her instructions to dry her milk and how to wean the child. The case worker drives them back to the foster home to work out arrangements for foster care for the baby. Four days later, the worker takes Mrs. Barnes to interview for jobs suggested by an Employment Agency. Since baby Kenneth enjoys riding in a car, the mother took him along too. Although most of the positions are filled, a café owner gives her hope by promising to call if he needs her.

On August 1, 1951, Gloria finds out that foster care can be obtained for the baby, providing her relatives are willing to pay $35 per month for care. The next day, a private contribution of $35 is made for the use of Mrs. Barnes. An agreement is signed between the mother and foster mother, who is willing to allow both mother and baby to remain there, until she can take the tests given by the Employment Office to qualify for a job. Nine days later, Mrs. Barnes leaves the baby at the foster home while she accepts a job as a Nurse's Aide in another county. She works with a practical nurse from August 10 to September 11, 1951. She receives praise from the nurse who states, "She was attentive and cooperative. She rendered good service under my guidance and supervision. I had the opportunity of observing her care and treatment of an elderly and critically ill patient. Mrs. Barnes only has a tenth grade education but feels she can overcome this limitation by application and a will to take advantage of the opportunity which she missed as a child." One week after that, baby Kenneth is examined by a Psychologist. Based on the results obtained in this one contact, it is determined that the child is adoptable. About a month later, September 14, 1951, Gloria's job in the neighboring county terminates and she is back at her father's home. Gloria has been dependent upon her family. She had never been able to make decisions for herself. Coming from an unstable home, (her father offers no stability to this girl or her children and he has been married three times) she has never been given the opportunity of decision making. She decides there is nothing for her to do but to surrender the child for adoption. Each time plans for the baby are mentioned, she says that she cannot keep the child. A Child Welfare Worker encourages her to talk about what she wants to do about the child, pointing out that it is "her" decision to make. She continues to say that she cannot take care of the baby and there was nothing else to do. Because of the "publicity" surrounding this case, Gloria (and her family) feels it is best for her to surrender her child in a Court outside of McNairy County. By November 7, 1951, Gloria Barnes has released her baby for adoption. On November 9, 1951, she signs the proper form, in the presence of a Circuit Judge, surrendering Kenneth Eugene for adoption. She recognized that she could not give Kenneth Eugene a fair chance at a normal life. Gloria is now attending a practical nursing course and is guaranteed a job with the completion of the course. Her plan is to finish the course, get a job, repay the student loan, establish a home, and ask the court to reopen the case and consider giving her the three children back. It is discovered, agreed upon, and notification has been made to the Department of Public Welfare in Nashville, Tennessee, that the children are being neglected, and are in an unsuitable situation with their father. At some point, the paternal grandfather has been given custody of the three children by Melzar Barnes.

On December 6, 1951, the Dept. of Public Welfare receives a request for a summary of Kenneth Eugene as the child is being considered for placement. A conference is held for the purpose of planning his presentation and placement with his adoptive parents. He will meet his adoptive parents on December 12, 1951. On December 14, 1951, Kenneth Eugene is removed from his foster home. When he sees his adoptive father, he went, without hesitation, to his arms, however, he turned his head to look back at the worker. He acted the same way when the adoptive mother first held him. Acceptance of each other was mutual. The adoptive parents indicated that they wanted the child almost immediately after they had seen him. The three of them left in a happy frame of mind.

Mrs. Barnes was interviewed on February 26, 1952 by a Tennessee Child Welfare worker. It was her day off from work. She rooms alone in a comfortable room which is located on the first floor of the hospital. The obstetrics is located just above her and, at first, the noise was disturbing to her. She worried a great deal over the condition of the patients but has begun to refrain from worrying so much. She is earning enough to repay the loan and wants to pay more, in order to repay her loan as soon as possible.

During the interview, Mrs. Barnes showed some anxiety about her family. She has not heard from her father since Christmas although she has written to him. Mrs. Barnes wrote to the Reverend Moore's wife and asked if her father still had her little girl, Vickie, age 3, but has not heard back from her. She expressed that she wished some plan could be made so that she could have her little girl with her. She showed concern about her twin boys, age 6, who are with her father-in-law. She felt that she was not given a fair chance to secure custody of them and Vickie. She seemed more interested in having Vickie with her than the other children. Mrs. Barnes showed resentment toward her stepmother and said that the last time she visited home, her stepmother said that she did not want to "hear tell of her" or see her again. She thinks the stepmother may have interfered with her father's writing to her.

Mrs. Barnes talked freely and seemed to appreciate the worker's visit and interest in her. Worker writes, "I feel that review of the case record would give me a better understanding of this situation and help us in continuing service to Mrs. Barnes. I would appreciate your mailing us this record."

I will give you a new heart and put a new spirit in you; I will remove from you your heart of stone and give you a heart of flesh. (Ez 36:26)

I can't explain Gloria's increased anxiety regarding the sudden need to know of her daughter's whereabouts. Maybe *she* was stricken with a sudden feeling of dread, and it turned out to be a "mother's intuition." While Gloria was writing letters home to her father, trying to get information about the child, the little girl had been taken and relocated to Texas. Gloria worked hard to establish a career, one that would enable her to reunite the family. That became her ultimate goal. In the process, she lost a baby boy and a three-year-old daughter. Unfortunately, it was one of those times when hard work and dedication could not overcome the negative odds stacked against her. While Gloria expressed concern about the twin boys, she must have had a sense of relief, knowing they were safe and being cared for by their paternal grandfather and his wife. That had been a mystery to me all my life. Why had they remained with family when I had been removed?

After receiving and reading Rodney's paperwork from the Tennessee Children's Welfare Department, I saw where custody of the three children was taken from their mother, Gloria, when she became "illegally" pregnant. However, she did not find out about the loss until a month after she gave birth to her son, Kenneth. That is when she received the court order that gave Melzar full custody. It had been done underhandedly, without her knowledge and without prior notification by the court or her ex-husband. In the court's defense, it is possible they might not have known Gloria's whereabouts. Due to her "illegal" condition (pregnant), she was living in a "foster care" facility.

Without the Welfare Department's documentation, I would never have known the three children lived in foster homes: the boys with one family and me with another. It saddened me to read where we were removed from those caring families and given to Melzar, without any sort of preparation for them, or for us. The Welfare Department papers said, "It was a tearful and traumatic experience."

Less than a year later, it was discovered the children were in an unsuitable situation. They were being neglected by their father. The Department of Public Welfare in Nashville, Tennessee, was notified.

Melzar Barnes gave custody of the three children to his father, their paternal grandfather. The discovery of that information does shed some light (although speculative) on a few previously unanswered statements and/or questions:

1. Aunt Doris told me, "One time, Big Daddy, (the grandfather) told Gloria, he could get me back if she wanted him to." That was probably about the time when Gloria and Dale visited me in Houston. They had been to Tennessee to get the boys from their grandfather and take them home, to Michigan. On the way, they stopped to see me. Perhaps they stopped to get me. Gloria's later response to him was, "she couldn't take me away from the only family I had ever known."

2. J. B. Barnes's "magic words" to gain entrance for Gloria to see me in Houston might have been "illegal adoption." Or did he know about the exchange for money?

3. It might explain the lack of an answer to the question I asked Mother, "Was I ever legally adopted?" How could the adoption have been legal (even though Gloria did sign papers) if custody had been removed from her? Melzar swore he never signed adoption papers. But then, why would he? He knew he had given custody of the children to his father. I highly doubt he obtained a "bill of sale" or a "receipt."

Perhaps finding the real answer to the $10,000 mystery question "Why had the twins remained with family members when I had been removed?" takes us all the way back to the beginning of this book: "Where does that red hair come from, Gloria?" One old belief about having a redheaded baby is: "With red hair being rare, a child born to non-redheaded parents was often assumed to be the child of an affair. Thus, the child was treated badly." Country folks *do* have their beliefs. Maybe we should take a closer look at this one. Future time and money might be saved if we really understood its potential toward accuracy. After all, DNA doesn't lie. Thus, we could consider this old belief regarding a redheaded child born to non-redheaded parents a proven fact, right?

Recently, I was watching the television show *Face the Nation* when I heard Paul Ryan: "The condition of your birth does not determine the outcome of your life." While that statement has proven itself to be true over and over again, I firmly believe it is absolutely necessary to have at least *one* person in your corner. That person must be someone who believes in you and is willing to offer and give help. Take, for an example, former president Obama. He continues to give credit to his grandmother for constantly being there for him. He always talks about what a remarkable influence she was on his life.

Gloria reached out for help on many occasions, but time and time again, she was denied. She wanted what was best for her children and suffered their loss silently throughout the years. After I read what that Tennessee Child Welfare worker had written, I felt as if I could better understand the situation. Her words took me to a place far back in time, sixty-four years ago. Although it is hard to imagine exactly what Gloria was going through, I tried to *see* it with all my senses, but mostly with my heart. I think it might have gone something like this:

It is February 25, 1952. There is no color; everything is black and white. The hospital is old, but it is clean with mixed sterile scents of alcohol and bleach. It is late at night, and the hospital is quiet. It is so silent that you can hear the swish of a stiffly starched and ironed nurse's uniform as she swiftly walks the hallway.

The skirt rubs against her pale leg of white nylon as she scurries down the long corridor to a patient's room. How many of these trips has she made today? She carries an old clipboard with a pen to take notes and update vitals. She finds the patient resting peacefully. *Good*, she thinks. But she hesitates there and takes just a moment to watch and envy that kind of peace. It is the kind of peacefulness that allows one to quietly drift off; worry free, guilt free.

Totally engrossed in her thoughts, she jumps when the silence is suddenly broken by the intrusive sound of her pen as it hits the floor. She glances at the patient, who remains undisturbed. She bends down to retrieve the item and notices an unacceptable runner in her new hosiery. In five more minutes, she will be off. It's not feasible to replace the damaged stocking now, although it is in strict violation of dress code. *More money*, she thinks. Her concern is not only about the money but also about receiving a warning, should an administrator notice the violation. She is following all the rules, working every possible hour, earning every dime to pay on the student loan. She wants to pay more than the monthly requirement so it can be paid off as quickly as possible. The sooner it is paid, the sooner her life can find a new beginning.

Today has been hard. She has worked a double shift, but looks forward to being off tomorrow. She has an interview with a Tennessee Child Welfare worker and hopes it will bring her one step closer to reuniting the family. If only she can get a good night's sleep before they talk. This meeting might be the most important one she will ever have. She wants to be alert; everything depends on it. The hospital is her home now, but it won't always be. The surroundings are not usually conducive to a good, restful night's sleep. The room they have provided is comfortable. She will tidy it up tonight, although nothing is out of place. It is located on the first floor.

She rooms alone. Sometimes alone is unbearably lonely and the silence can be deafening. That's when she spends some time with her old friend Zenith. She doesn't have a television and feels fortunate to at least have the radio. Her favorite time is anytime when Patti Page sings the "Tennessee Waltz."

She slips out of the uniform and pulls the elastic waistband of the long, half-slip up over her brassiere, and it is transformed into a sleek, straight, white gown, complete with spaghetti straps. The lace makes it elegant enough for a ball. Her stark, sterile cap becomes a tall, jeweled crown that brings out the beauty of her glistening black hair and highlights her lovely olive complexion. She dances around the room to the "Tennessee Waltz."

She glances at the mirror and comes to an abrupt stop, surprised by her own reflection. She sees a remarkable resemblance to a rising young star by the name of Elizabeth Taylor. Ah, but she shouldn't dare think that way. That's just the sort of thing that gets a young woman into trouble. She certainly couldn't justify any kind of self-admiration, not her. She must constantly remind herself of her ultimate goal. There is no time for daydreaming. She has to concentrate on one goal: work hard, earn money, find the three children who are left, and get them back.

There are those *other* times. Those are the times when the old Zenith can be her worst enemy, serving as a reminder of past transgressions. By now, the song on the radio has changed, and this new one indicates that tonight might be one of those unforgiving times. Johnny and the Four Lads croon their 1951 hit, "Cry."

The lyrics are about heartache and the blues, but suggest that the sun can still be found beyond a cloudy sky, finishing with "so let your hair down and go on and cry."

Once again, she finds it hard to sleep with the obstetrics located just above on the second floor. She thinks back. At first, the noise was so disturbing. She would show up for work with little to no rest, but she offered the others a good excuse: She "worries about the condition of the patients, the women in labor."

They didn't need to know the truth about *her* suffering. They didn't need to know how she cries herself to sleep most nights. Her concerns were for her *own* children. The physical labor pains couldn't compare to the agonizing emotional pain of losing all your children within the same nine-month time span it takes to conceive, carry, and deliver a child. She mourns the loss of her baby, gone forever. She can still smell the pure, sweet fragrance of his hair, see his trusting, innocent, loving smile, and sense the softness of his small, perfect body. When she hears the first cries of the newborns, she longs to comfort them, to hold them in her arms.

Gloria fears for her little girl. *Where is she?* Tomorrow she will ask the case worker for help. She will tell her of the many letters she has written to her father. He has not written back or tried to contact her since Christmas. She will tell her about writing to the pastor's wife and receiving no response. Could it be that they were all trying to hide something from her? Oh, that was probably just paranoia creeping in. She has made a firm decision to ask the case worker for help. The fact that a decision has been made at all represents remarkable progress for her. She needs to get permission to allow her daughter to stay with her. There are people who will be willing to babysit while she works. Surely the case worker would help. A little girl *needs* to be with her mother. She's certain the case worker will understand.

That night, despite the song, despite the cries of a woman in labor or those from her newborn baby, for the first time in a long time, Gloria is able to close her eyes and sleep peacefully. She has a plan.

The next day, the case worker patiently listens to her new client. She writes a request to the agency. She wishes to review the case for an overall better understanding of the entire situation. She asks that all Gloria's records be mailed to her so she may be of better service.

She is determined to help Gloria get her little girl so they can be together. Neither of them could have known—it was already too late.

Gloria never seemed to recover from the loss of her son, Jim, killed in Vietnam. His death led her into despair, which resulted in several years of depression. That can happen when one loses hope. I think Gloria finally pulled herself together enough to realize something well known: "Where there is life, there is hope."

Once she came to that realization, I choose to think she lived with a hope and a belief that someday, given the opportunity, she could possibly be reunited with Kenneth. Gloria never mentioned that to anyone. Why would she? She had been ostracized and ridiculed by family and society. The circumstances were different. By then, she knew where her daughter was, but she had no idea where the baby had been placed. I believe she made a private commitment to herself that someday she would find the baby she felt forced to give up. After all, she had chosen to remain a part of her daughter's life, no matter how minuscule. Without encouragement of any kind, she continued to send cards, letters, and gifts; attended her graduation; and spent any amount of time with her that she possibly could.

I am thankful that time was kind to both of us. It allowed me to really get to know this woman who gave birth to four children—and while still very young—ended up with only one.

I know how strong she was. She was an over comer. Like John Wayne, she managed to kick cancer's butt several times. She overcame devastating life events and losses while she suffered silently. She cherished each moment spent with her children as though they were precious gifts. She loved deeply and unconditionally.

Throughout the years when we talked on the telephone, I could hear smiles in her voice. She spoke lovingly and compassionately of her friends and displayed gentleness and kindness toward her pets. As time went on, the old of each gave way to the new. I never had the honor of getting to know most of them, but I saw pictures of many.

I read captions on backs of photos. The words let me know of their importance and how much they were loved. How much *more* must she have loved her son?

There was a time when I couldn't have understood Gloria's actions, a time when I took it all so personally: "If my own birth mother gave me away, who could love me?" I felt incredible rejection: unloved, unlovable, bitter, and unhappy. Those feelings can create such emotional turmoil. If allowed, they can literally destroy a person. I had quite a pity party and knew nothing about the truth or the power of forgiveness and how both bring so much freedom and peace.

Troy Dunn, on TV's *The Locator*, states, "You can't find peace until you find all the pieces." While my life continues to be a puzzle with one large missing piece, the picture is no longer distorted the way it once was. The decision to research my past enriched my life. It enabled me to move forward, both psychologically and emotionally.

I would like to know who my birth father is. The information could give me more insight. It would enable me to learn more about the feelings and emotions of those persons involved, those who may have been greatly affected by the unintentional intertwining of our lives. That would allow for an even better understanding of the situation. The final piece, as with any puzzle, is significant. It would bring the entire picture together.

I have discovered that one of the most important aspects of learning the circumstances of my past is that I have begun to heal the brokenness. I learned that I was not "unwanted," so I have a much greater feeling of self-worth and self-esteem. I discovered there were many people who wanted to keep me: Aunt Doris, the minister's brother and his wife, Archie and Vinnie, Virginia, a foster family (who I wish I could remember), my mom and dad—the Faulkners, and Gloria. The ability to add Gloria's name to the list was a welcome surprise in my findings. It was very important for me to find out how hard she tried to keep her family together. My fear of rejection is no longer the major issue it once was. That in itself is a great victory.

More than once, I've heard Pastor Joel Osteen say, "Sometimes God has to take time to grow you up." That used to confuse me (given my age). In the last few years, as I entered senior citizen status, I began to (worry that He might run out of time on me) understand that growing-up doesn't necessarily have anything to do with one's age. I had to begin by acknowledging that there are missing pieces in my life and overcome the fear that what we don't know can sometimes hurt us more than what we do know — and the other way around. Yes, 'fear' can send you running in a circle. I had to pray with an open mind and heart for the Lord to protect me and at the same time, reveal truth in all things. Through faith, I asked the Lord to give me strength and wisdom to understand what he would reveal and how to use the information wisely. I realized that this prayer could be demanding on my part. It would probably include a willingness to ask difficult questions, get answers, and face the truth about things that are hard to accept, hard to understand, and even harder to discuss. I've learned that life's circumstances—whether good, bad, sad, surprising, shocking, intense, emotional, funny, or even hilarious—allow us the opportunity, time and information needed to help us grow. Without my stretching and growing-up period, which came from deep within my soul, I could never have begun to understand what Pastor Joel meant. Undeniably, the best and most rewarding part of my growing-up, or discovery journey wasn't about "finding out who I am." It wasn't about *me* at all. The best part was finding someone else to love: my brother. And maybe it has helped someone else along the way.

"… and I say to myself, what a wonderful world …
oh yeah."

"For I know the plans I have for you," declares the Lord, "plans to prosper you and not to harm you, plans to give you hope and a future." (Jer 29:11)

The End

ACKNOWLEDGMENTS

Thank you, heavenly Father, for placing this challenging project on my heart.

Thanks to my grandchildren: Jordan, who said, "Nana, you should write a book!" And to Peyton, who helped me title it.

My friends and family: Thank you to my "retired" friend, Valerie, for working beyond the call of duty, and to my lifelong friends Carol and Judy, for listening beyond the call of duty. Loving appreciation to Bud, Jim, and Stefanie, and to all my brothers and sister(s): Evelyn, J.L., Billy, Harold and Carol, and Rodney. I love you all.

Thank you for being there, Aunt Doris. I hope all my new Tennessee and Mississippi friends and relatives (alias Cousins by the Dozens) will find something of value in this little book of my life.

Special thanks to my friend Clive Warner and the talented writers at CC, especially to "Quiv"—write it, and they will read.

Thanks to the professional staff at iUniverse for their help.

Thank you, Coach Mark, for your immeasurable advice, encouragement, patience, and understanding.

SOURCES

Newton County, MS, NCMHGS Archives, Cooper, TANN, "STOLEN BABIES."

Jett, "Tann: Matron of Evil" @ criminalelement.com.

Ramond, *Baby Thief.* 1–322.

Poppy, "Woman Stole children from Poor to give to Rich."

Pope Francis, "2015—Sudden Loss of a Loved One."

"48 Hours: Hard Evidence," January 18, 2016, 9:08 p.m., "Ghost Story for South Texas."

Eastman, *Are You My Mother?* 3–72.

Mendoza, *We Do Not Die Alone.* 6–126.

Gray, *More Stories for the Heart.*175.

Mehl, *More Stories for the Heart.* 269.

LaPell, Greatest Gun Fights: Hamilton Draws on Pusser @ guns.com.

Hawthorne, *Scarlet Letter.* 64.

Paul Ryan, May, 2015, *Face the Nation*, comments on condition of birth, "outcome of life."

Printed in the United States
By Bookmasters